SOUNDER

WILLIAM H. ARMSTRONG

WITH

CONNECTIONS

HOLT, RINEHART AND WINSTON
Harcourt Brace & Company

Austin • New York • Orlando • Atlanta • San Francisco
Boston • Dallas • Toronto • London

For permission to reprint copyrighted material, grateful acknowledgment is made to the following sources:

HarperCollins Publishers: Sounder by William H. Armstrong. Copyright © 1969 by William H. Armstrong.

F. E. Albi: "Moco Limping" by David Nava Monreal. *Arte Público Press:* "The Smartest Human I Ever Met: My Brother's Dog Shep" from *Walking Stars* by Victor Villaseñor. Copyright © 1994 by Victor Villaseñor. Published by Arte Público Press—University of Houston, 1994. *Bantam Doubleday Dell Books for Young Readers:* "Lob's Girl" from *A Whisper in the Night* by Joan Aiken. Copyright © 1984 by Joan Aiken. *Harvard University Press:* "Chapter VII" from *The Narrative of the Life of Frederick Douglass,* edited by Benjamin Quarles. Copyright © 1960 and renewed © 1988 by the President and Fellows of Harvard College. Published by Harvard University Press, Cambridge, MA. *Simon & Schuster Books for Young Readers, an imprint of Simon & Schuster Children's Publishing Division:* "Spirits of the Railway" from *Tales from Gold Mountain* by Paul Yee. Copyright © 1989 by Paul Yee. *Warner Bros. Publications U.S. Inc., Miami, FL 33014:* Lyrics from "I Believe I Can Fly" by R. Kelly. Copyright © 1996 by Zomba Songs Inc./R. Kelly Publishing, Inc. All rights reserved.

To Kip, Dave, and Mary

"*A man keeps, like his love, his courage dark.*"

—*Antoine de Saint Exupéry*

Also by William H. Armstrong

SOUR LAND

Contents

Sounder, by William H. Armstrong 1

Connections 117

Lob's Girl (short story)   by Joan Aiken 119

The Smartest Human I Ever Met: My Brother's Dog Shep
(short story)   by Victor Villaseñor 133

Moco Limping (poem)   by David Nava Monreal 137

Spirits of the Railway (short story)   by Paul Yee 139

Learning to Read and Write   (memoir)
from *The Narrative of the Life of Frederick Douglass,*
by Frederick Douglass 144

Lonesome Valley (spiritual) 152

I Believe I Can Fly (song)   by R. Kelly 153

David and Goliath (reader's theater)
from I Samuel 17, adapted by Diane B. Engel 155

William H. Armstrong (biographical sketch) 160

Author's Note

FIFTY YEARS AGO I learned to read at a round table in the center of a large, sweet-smelling, steam-softened kitchen. My teacher was a gray-haired black man who taught the one-room Negro school several miles away from where we lived in the Green Hill district of the county. He worked for my father after school and in the summer. There were no radios or television sets, so when our lessons were finished he told us stories. His stories came from Aesop, the Old Testament, Homer, and history.

There was a lasting, magnificent intoxication about the man that has remained after half a century. There was seldom a preacher at the white-washed, clapboard Baptist church in the Green Hill district, so he came often to our white man's church and sat alone in the balcony. Sometimes the minister would call on this eloquent, humble man to lead the congregation in prayer. He would move quietly to the foot of the balcony steps, pray with the simplicity of the Carpenter of Nazareth, and then return to where he sat alone, for no other black people ever came to join him.

He had come to our community from farther south, already old when he came. He talked little, or not at all, about his past. But one night at the great center table after he had told the story of Argus, the faithful dog of Odysseus, he told the story of Sounder, a coon dog.

It is the black man's story, not mine. It was not from Aesop, the Old Testament, or Homer. It was history—*his* history.

That world of long ago has almost totally changed. The church balcony is gone. The table is gone from the kitchen. But the story remains.

W. H. ARMSTRONG

SOUNDER

I

THE TALL MAN stood at the edge of the porch. The roof sagged from the two rough posts which held it, almost closing the gap between his head and the rafters. The dim light from the cabin window cast long equal shadows from man and posts. A boy stood nearby shivering in the cold October wind. He ran his fingers back and forth over the broad crown of the head of a coon dog named Sounder.

1

"Where did you first get Sounder?" the boy asked.

"I never got him. He came to me along the road when he wasn't more'n a pup."

The father turned to the cabin door. It was ajar. Three small children, none as high as the level of the latch, were peering out into the dark. "We just want to pet Sounder," the three all said at once.

"It's too cold. Shut the door."

"Sounder and me must be about the same age," the boy said, tugging gently at one of the coon dog's ears, and then the other. He felt the importance of the years—as a child measures age— which separated him from the younger children. He was old enough to stand out in the cold and run his fingers over Sounder's head.

No dim lights from other cabins punctuated the night. The white man who owned the vast endless fields had scattered the cabins of his Negro sharecroppers far apart, like flyspecks on a whitewashed ceiling. Sometimes on Sundays the boy walked with his parents to set awhile at one of the distant cabins. Sometimes they went to the meetin' house. And there was school too. But it was far away at the edge of town. Its term began after harvest and ended before planting time.

2

Two successive Octobers the boy had started, walking the eight miles morning and evening. But after a few weeks when cold winds and winter sickness came, his mother had said, "Give it up, child. It's too long and too cold." And the boy, remembering how he was always laughed at for getting to school so late, had agreed. Besides, he thought, next year he would be bigger and could walk faster and get to school before it started and wouldn't be laughed at. And when he wasn't dead-tired from walking home from school, his father would let him hunt with Sounder. Having both school and Sounder would be mighty good, but if he couldn't have school, he could always have Sounder.

"There ain't no dog like Sounder," the boy said. But his father did not take up the conversation. The boy wished he would. His father stood silent and motionless. He was looking past the rim of half-light that came from the cabin window and pushed back the darkness in a circle that lost itself around the ends of the cabin. The man seemed to be listening. But no sounds came to the boy.

Sounder was well named. When he treed a coon or possum in a persimmon tree or on a wild-grape vine, his voice would roll across the flatlands. It wavered through the foothills, louder than any other dog's in the whole countryside.

What the boy saw in Sounder would have been totally missed by an outsider. The dog was not much to look at—a mixture of Georgia redbone hound and bulldog. His ears, nose, and color were those of a redbone. The great square jaws and head, his muscular neck and broad chest showed his bulldog blood. When a possum or coon was shaken from a tree, like a flash Sounder would clamp and set his jaw-vise just behind the animal's head. Then he would spread his front paws, lock his shoulder joints, and let the bulging neck muscles fly from left to right. And that was all. The limp body, with not a torn spot or a tooth puncture in the skin, would be laid at his master's feet. His master's calloused hand would rub the great neck, and he'd say "Good Sounder, good Sounder." In the winter when there were no crops and no pay, fifty cents for a possum and two dollars for a coonhide bought flour and overall jackets with blanket linings.

But there was no price that could be put on Sounder's voice. It came out of the great chest cavity and broad jaws as though it had bounced off the walls of a cave. It mellowed into half-echo before it touched the air. The mists of the flatlands strained out whatever coarseness was left

4

over from his bulldog heritage, and only flutelike redbone mellowness came to the listener. But it was louder and clearer than any purebred redbone. The trail barks seemed to be spaced with the precision of a juggler. Each bark bounced from slope to slope in the foothills like a rubber ball. But it was not an ordinary bark. It filled up the night and made music as though the branches of all the trees were being pulled across silver strings.

While Sounder trailed the path the hunted had taken in search of food, the high excited voice was quiet. The warmer the trail grew, the longer the silences, for, by nature, the coon dog would try to surprise his quarry and catch him on the ground, if possible. But the great voice box of Sounder would have burst if he had tried to trail too long in silence. After a last, long-sustained stillness which allowed the great dog to close in on his quarry, the voice would burst forth so fast it overflowed itself and became a melody.

A stranger hearing Sounder's treed bark suddenly fill the night might have thought there were six dogs at the foot of one tree. But all over the countryside, neighbors, leaning against slanting porch posts or standing in open cabin doorways and listening, knew that it was Sounder.

"If the wind does not rise, I'll let you go hunting with me tonight." The father spoke quietly as he glanced down at boy and dog. "Animals don't like to move much when it's windy."

"Why?" the boy asked.

"There are too many noises, and they can't hear a killer slipping up on them. So they stay in their dens, especially possums, because they can't smell much."

The father left the porch and went to the woodpile at the edge of the rim of light. The boy followed, and each gathered a chunk-stick for the cabin stove. At the door, the father took down a lantern that hung on the wall beside a possum sack and shook it. "There's plenty of coal oil," he said.

The boy closed the door quickly. He had heard leaves rattling across the frozen ground. He hoped his father didn't hear it. But he knew the door wouldn't shut it out. His father could sense the rising wind, and besides, it would shake the loose windowpanes.

Inside the cabin, the boy's mother was cutting wedge-shaped pieces of corn mush from an iron pot that stood on the back of the stove. She browned them in a skillet and put them on the tin-topped table in the middle of the room. The boy and the three younger children ate their sup-

6

per in silence. The father and mother talked a little about ordinary things, talk the boy had heard so many times he no longer listened. "The crop will be better next year. There'll be more day work. The hunting was better last year."

This winter the hunting was getting worse and worse. The wind came stronger and colder than last year. Sometimes Sounder and his master hunted in the wind. But night after night they came home with an empty brown sack. Coons were scarcely seen at all. People said they had moved south to the big water. There were few scraps and bones for Sounder. Inside the cabin, they were hungry for solid food too. Corn mush had to take the place of stewed possum, dumplings, and potatoes.

Not long after supper, Sounder's master went out of the cabin and stood listening, as he always did, to see if he could hear the cold winter wind beginning to rise in the hills. When he came back into the cabin, he took off his blanket-lined overall jacket and sat behind the stove for a long time. Sounder whined at the door as if he were asking if someone had forgotten to light the lantern and start across the fields of dead stalks to the lowlands or past the cottonwoods and jack oaks to the hills. The boy took Sounder some table scraps in a tin pan. As Sounder licked the bottom of the pan it rattled against a loose board in the porch as if somebody were walking across the floor.

Later, when it was time for the smaller children in the cabin to go to bed, Sounder's master got up, put on his overall jacket, and went outside. He did not take the lantern or Sounder or the boy with him. The stern order to the coon hound to go back under the porch came in through the cabin door, and Sounder's whining continued long after the footsteps on the frozen path had died out.

Inside the cabin, the boy's mother sat by the stove, picking kernels of walnuts with a bent hairpin. The woman watched each year for the walnuts to fall after the first hard frost. Each day she went with the children and gathered all that had fallen. The brownish-green husks, oozing their dark purple stain, were beaten off on a flat rock outside the cabin. On the same rock, the nuts were cracked after they had dried for several weeks in a tin box under the stove. When kernel-picking time came, before it was dark each day, the boy or the father took a hammer with a home-made handle, went to the flat rock, and cracked as many as could be kerneled in a night.

The troubled whimper of a child came through the little door that led to the shed-room where the children slept.

"You must go to bed soon," the mother said. "Your little brother gets addled in his sleep when you ain't in bed with him."

The boy reached into his mother's lap, where the golden half-kernels lay in the folds of her apron. She slapped his hand away. "You eat the crumbs from the bottom of the hull basket," she said. "I try to pick two pounds a night. That's thirty cents' worth. Fifteen cents a pound at the store if they're mostly half-kernels and dry. The man won't pay if they're all in crumbs."

Sometimes the woman told the boy stories she had heard at the meetin' house. "The Lord do powerful things" she would say. The boy liked it when she told her stories. They took away night loneliness. Night loneliness was always bad when the younger children had gone to bed, or when the father was not in the cabin. "Night loneliness is part fearing," the boy's mother had once said to him. But the boy was never afraid when his father was near.

Perhaps she too felt the loneliness that came with the wind as it passed the cabin outside, and the closeness of a world whose farthest border in

9

the night was the place where the lamp light ended, at the edge of the cabin walls. So she told the boy a story of a mighty flood which the Lord had sent to wash away all the evil in the world. When the story was over, she sent the boy to bed and continued picking out kernels and adding them to the neat mound in the folds of her apron.

The boy pressed his head deep into his straw pillow. The pillow was cold, but it felt smooth, and it smelled fresh. He had the same feeling he got when he rubbed his face against the sheets that hung on the clothesline every Monday. His mother washed his pillowcase and sheet every week, just like she did for the people who lived in the big house down the road. He buried himself deep in his side of the straw tick; he felt where the wooden slats of the bed crossed under his body. He rolled close to his little brother and tucked the edge of the coverlet under his body to keep out the cold that seeped up through the straw ticking. His little brother's body warmed him.

He heard Sounder whimpering under the porch. But Sounder was warm because the boy's father had put two burlap sacks under the porch for the time when the hard frosts came. The boy thought there must be two pounds of nuts in the

10

pile on his mother's lap. His mother always said "Two pounds is a good night's work if you can start early and there ain't a sick child to rock."

He wondered where his father had gone without Sounder; they always went together at night. He heard the thump, thump, thump of Sounder's paw hitting the underneath side of the porch floor as he scratched at a flea in his short tan hair.

The boy dreamed of the stalk land covered by the Lord's mighty flood. He wondered where the animals would go if the water rose over the foothills. "Cabins built on posts would just float like boats, porch and all," he assured himself in a whisper. If they floated from the far ends of the land and all came together, that would be a town, and he wouldn't be lonely anymore . . .

* * *

When the boy awoke in the morning, he went to the window. He remembered his dream of the flood covering the stalk land. He called the younger children. His breath steamed up the windowpane. He wiped the steam away with the bottom of his fist. His dream had not come true. There was no floodwater rising in the bottom-

11

land. Except for frost on the ground, everything looked just the same as it had yesterday. The younger children looked, saw nothing, and asked, "What is it?"

The big blue-enameled possum kettle was boiling on top of the chunk stove. It had two lids and doubled for cooking and heating. The boy felt the brown paper bag of walnut kernels on the shelf behind the stove. "Yes," he said to his mother, "I think there are two pounds."

He stood close to the warm stovepipe, turning one cheek and then the other to its glowing warmth. He circled his arms in a wide embrace around the pipe and rubbed his hands together. The warmth ran up his sleeves and down over his ribs inside his shirt and soaked inward through his whole body. He pulled in deep breaths from above the stove to catch the steam escaping from under the kettle's lid as it bounced up and down, breaking the rhythm of the bubbles that went *lob, lob, lob* on the surface of the fast-boiling pot.

In a skillet on the second stove lid there were pork sausages! He sniffed the thin lines of smoke curling up from under the edges of each of them. Pork sausage was for Christmas. But he knew it wasn't Christmas yet. His mother put a pan of cold biscuits on the lid of the possum kettle to warm. She was humming to herself. The lid stopped jumping up and down, and the steam began to whistle softly as it squeezed from under the lid.

The smell that came from under the lid wasn't possum. It was ham bone. The boy had only smelled it twice in his life, once before in his own cabin, and once when he was walking past the big house down the road. The sausage and ham-bone smells filled up the cabin and leaked out through the cracks in the floor and around the door. They excited Sounder, and now he was scratching at the door.

Sounder hadn't had much to eat yesterday. Besides a few scraps, he had had one cold biscuit. When flour was scarce, the boy's mother would wrap the leftover biscuits in a clean flour sack and put them away for the next meal. Then they would be put in a pan, sprinkled with a little water to keep them soft, and warmed over. The boy called to Sounder to stop and go away. His mother stopped her humming and said, "Shush, child, you'll wake your father."

Then she went back to her humming. His mother always hummed when she was worried. When she held a well child on her lap and rocked back and forth, she sang. But when she held a sick child close in her arms and the rocker moved just enough to squeak a little, she would hum. Sometimes she hummed so softly that the child heard the deep concerned breathing of terror above the sound of the humming. The boy always thought her lips looked as though they were glued together when she hummed. They seemed to be rolled inward and drawn long and thin. Once when she kissed him good night when he was sick, they were cold, he remembered. But when she sang or told stories, her lips were rolled out, big and warm and soft.

Outside, the wind still blew, the sun was weak, and the earth was gray. Several times the boy went out to bring wood for his mother. He ate sausage and biscuits at the tin-topped table with the other children.

When his father got up, he chopped some wood and sat by the fire. The top of the possum kettle bounced up and down again because the biscuit pan had been moved. The father lifted the lid now and then. With the big wire fork that had a wooden handle, he pulled the ham half out of the water and turned it over. The boy felt warm and proud inside when he saw his father's great hand take hold of the handle of the hot lid without using a pot rag the way his mother always did. Finally his father took from the shelf a flat

14

oak slab, bigger than any of the pans or dishes, and put it on the table.

The boy liked to smell the oak slab. It smelled like the Mercy Seat meetin'-house picnic held every summer. He also liked to rub his fingers on the edge of the slab, for it was soft and smooth where the grease had soaked it. His father had hollowed it out during long winter evenings as he sat by the stove. The boy had cleaned up the shavings and slipped them under the door of the stove when the draft was open. They burned with a bright flame, and they made a great mystery for the boy: The curled ones straightened out as they burned, but the straight ones curled up.

The boy remembered when the oak slab had had ham on it before. One year his father had won a pig in a shooting match and raised it to a hog. They had eaten one ham and traded one for beans and flour at the store. That year they had spareribs and chitlins and pan scrapple. Sometimes when the boy's father helped butcher hogs down at the big house, he would bring home spareribs and sowbelly—lots of sowbelly, but not much spareribs.

The boy's father took the ham from the kettle and put it on the oak slab. "Save the ham-boilin' for Sounder," he reminded the boy's mother.

"Sounder will eat good now," the boy said.

15

The father sharpened the butcher knife with the whetstone he used to whet his scythe and his goose-necked brier hook in the summer when he cut brambles and young sumac in the fencerows. He cut big pieces of ham, and they stuck out from under the brown tops of the biscuits. It was like a Christmas bigger than a pork-sausage Christmas. The boy slipped a piece of the fat rind into a biscuit and took it out to Sounder. When the ham-boiling had cooled, he filled Sounder's pan and ran his fingers up and down the great dog's back as he lapped it up.

The windows of the cabin stayed steamed up almost all day, the kettle had boiled so long. The cold wind continued to blow outside. Nothing moved except what the wind moved—dead leaves under the cabin, brown blades and stalks from the fields which were dead and ready to be blown away, bare branches of poplars, and the spires of tall pines. Toward evening the father wiped the steam away from the glass and looked out a couple of times. The dry cottonwood chunks burned like gunpowder in the stove. In one or two spots the side of the stove gave off a red glow.

With the flavor of ham and biscuit still in his mouth, the boy felt good. He watched his mother as she patched his father's overalls with a piece of ticking. The combination of faded blue overall cloth and gray-and-white-striped ticking looked odd. One time at the meetin'-house picnic, boys with patches the same color as their overalls had laughed at him and pointed to the checkered gingham on the knees of his overalls. He had felt mad and hurt. But his mother had said, "Pay no mind, child," and had led him away. He hoped no one would laugh at his father. His father wouldn't be hurt. He didn't get hurt. He would get mad and fight back, and the boy was always afraid when his father got mad.

When the woman had patched the torn place, she got the walnut basket, folded her apron in her lap, and began to pick out the golden-brown kernels. The boy thought she would sing, but the rocker only moved enough to squeak. She hummed softly, and her lips looked glued together. "Look down, look down that lonesome road." The boy wished she would stop humming and tell a story about the Lord or King David, but she kept humming "That Lonesome Road."

The boy decided it was lonesomer in bed in the dark than it was staying up. He was glad he could set a long time after the young children had gone to bed. Once he had been gathering weeds which his father had cut at the edge of a lawn. On the lawn a lady sat under a tree reading a story aloud to some children. He wished his mother or father could read. And if they had a book, he would hold the lamp by the chair so they could see the words and never get tired. "One day I will learn to read," he said to himself. He would have a book with stories in it, then he wouldn't be lonesome even if his mother didn't sing.

II

THE ROAD WHICH passed the cabin lay like a thread dropped on a patchwork quilt. Stalk land, fallow fields, and brushland, all appeared to be sewn together by wide fencerow stitches of trees. Their bare branches spread out to join together the separate patches of land. Weeds grew on either side of the road in summer, and a thin strip of green clung to life between the dusty tracks. In summer a horse and wagon made almost no noise in the

19

soft earth. In winter when the ground was frozen, the rattle of wheels and each distinct hoofbeat punctuated the winter quiet. When the wind blew, little clouds of dust would rise in the road and follow the wind tracks across the fields.

The boy was allowed to go as far as he wanted to on the road. But the younger children couldn't go past the pine clump toward the big house and the town, or the bramble patch where they picked blackberries in summer in the other direction. Almost no one passed on the road in winter except to buy flour at the store far down the road or to go to the town of a Saturday. Even in summer a speck on the horizon was a curiosity. People sitting on cabin porches would wonder whether the speck would take the form of man, woman, or child.

The third day after the boy had awakened to the smell of ham bone and pork sausage, it was still cold and the wind still blew. But the cabin still smelled good, and there was plenty to eat. Just as dark was gathering, the boy started to go to the woodpile to bring in wood for the night. The dim light of the lamp ran past the boy as he stood motionless in the open cabin door.

"Shut the door," the boy's father called from where he sat near the stove. But the boy did not move.

Just past the edge of the porch three white men stood in the dim light. Their heavy boots rattled the porch floor, and the boy backed quickly into the cabin as they pushed their way in.

"There are two things I can smell a mile," the first man said in a loud voice. "One's a ham cookin' and the other's a thievin' nigger."

"Get up," the second man ordered. The warm, but frozen circle of man, woman, and three small children around the stove jumped to their feet. A stool on which a child had been sitting fell backward and made a loud noise. One of the men kicked it across the room. The boy did not move from his place just inside the door.

"Here's the evidence," said the first man. He jerked at the grease-spotted cloth on the tin-topped table. The oak slab and the half-eaten ham fell to the floor with a great thud and slid against the wall.

"You know who I am," said the first man as he unbuttoned his heavy brown coat and pulled it back to show a shiny metal star pinned to his vest. "These are my deputies." The stranger nearest the door kicked it shut and swore about the cold.

"Stick out your hands, boy," ordered the second man. The boy started to raise his hands, but the man was already reaching over the stove, snapping handcuffs on the outstretched wrists of his father.

The click of the handcuffs was like the click of a gate latch at the big house where the boy had once gone with his father to work. He had swung on the gate and played with the latch until some-one had called out from the house, "If you want to swing on a gate, boy, swing on the one behind the house. Get away from the front."

The third stranger, who had not spoken, turned toward the door. "I'll bring up the wagon." But he did not open the door.

Suddenly the voice of the great dog shattered the heavy, seemingly endless silence that came between the gruff words of the sheriff and those of his men. Sounder was racing toward the cabin from the fields. He had grown restless from wait-ing to go hunting with his master and had wan-dered away to hunt alone. That's why he hadn't warned them. He always barked and sometimes, even in daytime, he would start from under the porch, the hair on his back straightening before anyone had sighted a moving speck at the far end of the road. "Somebody's comin' or a creature's movin'" the boy's mother would say.

Now he was growling and scratching at the door. The noise seemed to undo the fearful shock that had held the smaller children ashen and motionless. The youngest child began to cry and hid behind his mother. He tugged at her apron, but the woman did not move.

The men were speaking roughly to Sounder's master. "That tear in your overalls where the striped ticking is—that's where you tore them on the door hook of the smokehouse. We found threads of torn cloth in the hook. You gonna wear nothing but stripes pretty soon. Big, wide black and white stripes. Easy to hit with a shotgun."

The deputy who had started out to bring up the wagon kicked the closed door and swore at the dog on the other side.

"Go out and hold that mongrel if you don't want him shot." He held the door ajar the width of the boy's body and thrust him out. The boy fell on the back of the dog, whose snarling jaws had pushed into the light between the boy's legs. A heavy boot half pushed, half kicked the entangled feet of the sprawled boy and the nose of the dog and slammed the door. "Get that dog out of the way and hold him if you don't want him dead."

The boy, regaining his balance, dragged Sounder off the porch and to the corner of the cabin. Then the deputy, hearing the barking move back from the door, opened it and came out. He walked out of the circle of light but returned soon leading a horse hitched to a spring wagon. A saddled horse followed behind the wagon.

The appearance of the horses and the added confusion of people coming from the cabin roused Sounder to new fury. The boy felt his knees give. His arms ached, and his grip on the dog's collar was beginning to feel clammy and wet. But he held on.

"Chain him up," said the sheriff.

The boy thought they were telling him to chain up Sounder, but then he saw that one of the men had snapped a long chain on the handcuffs on his father's wrists. As the men pushed his father into the back of the wagon his overalls caught on the end of the tail-gate bolt, and he tore a long hole in his overalls. The bolt took one side of the ticking patch with it. The man holding the chain jerked it, and the boy's father fell backward into the wagon. The man swung the loose end of the chain, and it struck the boy's father across the face. One of the deputies pulled the chain tight and tied it to the wagon seat. The two deputies climbed on the wagon seat; the sheriff mounted the saddled horse. The cabin door was open; the boy's mother was standing in the doorway. He did not see his brother and sisters.

Sounder was making an awful noise, a half-strangled mixture of growl and bark. The boy spoke to him, but the great paws only dug harder to grip the frozen earth. Inch by inch the boy was losing his footing. Numbness was beginning to creep up his arms and legs, and he was being dragged away from the corner of the house.

The wagon started, and the sheriff rode behind it on his horse. Sounder made a great lunge forward, and the boy fell against the corner of the porch. Sounder raced after the wagon. No one yelled after him. The mother stood still in the doorway. The deputy who wasn't holding the reins turned on the seat, aimed his shotgun at the dog jumping at the side of the wagon, and fired. Sounder fell in the road, and the sheriff rode around him. Sounder's master was still on his back in the wagon, but he did not raise his head to look back.

The boy struggled to his feet. His head hurt where he had hit it against the corner of the porch. Now his mother spoke for the first time since he had opened the door to bring in wood. "Come in, child, and bring some wood."

Sounder lay still in the road. The boy wanted to cry; he wanted to run to Sounder. His stomach felt sick; he didn't want to see Sounder. He sank to his knees at the woodpile. His foot hurt where the door had been slammed on it. He thought he would carry in two chunk-sticks. Maybe his mother would drag Sounder out of the road. Maybe she would drag him across the fields and bury him. Maybe if she laid him on the porch and put some soft rags under him tonight, he might rise from the dead, like Lazarus did in a meetin'-house story. Maybe his father didn't know Sounder was dead. Maybe his father was dead in the back of the sheriff's wagon now. Maybe his father had said it hurt to bounce over the rough road on his back, and the deputy had turned around on the seat and shot him.

The second chunk-stick was too big. It slipped out of the boy's arms. Two of his fingers were bruised under the falling wood.

Suddenly a sharp yelp came from the road. Just like when a bee stung Sounder under the porch or a brier caught his ear in the bramble, the boy thought. In an instant the boy was on his feet. Bruised foot and fingers, throbbing head were forgotten. He raced into the dark. Sounder tried to rise but fell again. There was another yelp, this one constrained and plaintive. The boy, trained in night-sight when the lantern was dimmed so as not to alert the wood's creatures, picked out a blurred shape in the dark.

Sounder was running, falling, floundering, rising. The hind part of his body stayed up and moved from side to side, trying to lift the front part from the earth. He twisted, fell, and heaved his great shoulders. His hind paws dug into the earth. He pushed himself up. He staggered forward, sideways, then fell again. One front leg did not touch the ground. A trail of blood, smeared and blotted, followed him. There was a large spot of mingled blood, hair, and naked flesh on one shoulder. His head swung from side to side. He fell again and pushed his body along with his hind legs. One side of his head was a mass of blood. The blast had torn off the whole side of his head and shoulder.

The boy was crying and calling Sounder's name. He ran backward in front of Sounder. He held out his hand. Sounder did not make a sign to stop. The boy followed the coon dog under the porch, but he went far back under the cabin. The boy was on his knees, crying and calling, "Sounder, Sounder, Sound . . ." His voice trailed off into a pleading whisper.

The cabin door opened, and the boy's mother stood in the door. The pale light of the lamp inside ran past the woman, over the edge of the porch, and picked out the figure of the boy on his hands and knees. "Come in, child," the woman said. "He is only dying."

Inside the cabin the younger children sat huddled together near the stove. The boy rubbed his hands together near the stovepipe to warm them. His bruised fingers began to throb again. His foot and his head hurt, and he felt a lump rising on the side of his head. If Sounder would whimper or yelp, I would know, the boy thought. But there was no sound, no thump, thump, thump of a paw scratching fleas and hitting the floor underneath.

"Creatures like to die alone," the mother said after a long time. "They like to crawl away where nobody can find them dead, especially dogs. He didn't want to be shot down like a dog in the road. Some creatures are like people."

The road, the boy thought. What would it be like? Did the shotgun blast a hole in the road?

"I ain't got the wood," the boy said at last. "I'll light the lantern and get it."

"You know where the wood is. You won't need the lantern," the woman said.

The boy paused in the doorway. Then he took the lantern from the nail where it hung beside the possum sack. He took the lantern to the stove, lit a splinter of kindling through the open door-draft, and held it to the lantern wick the way his father always did. His mother said nothing to him. She spoke to the younger children instead. "I ain't fed you yet."

When he got outside, the boy did not go to the woodpile. He followed the trail of blood in its zig-zag path along the road. At the end of it there was a great wide spot, dark on the frozen ground. Little clumps of Sounder's hair lay in the blood. There was no hole where the shotgun had blasted. At the edge of the dark stain, the boy touched his finger to something. It was more than half of Sounder's long thin ear. The boy shivered and moved his finger away. He had seen dead lizards and possums and raccoons, but he'd never seen a human animal, like Sounder, dead.

It wouldn't work, he thought. But people always said to put things under your pillow when you go to bed, and if you make a wish, it will come true. He touched Sounder's ear again. It was cold. He picked it up. One edge of it was bloody, and jagged like the edge of a broken windowpane. He followed the zigzag trail back along the road, but he could scarcely see it now. He was crying again. At the corner of the porch he took the possum sack from the nail where it hung and wiped the ear. It gave him the shivers. He jumped down quickly, and holding the lantern near the ground, tried to see under the porch. He called Sounder. There was no sound. He went back to wiping the ear. His throat hurt. He put

30

the ear in the pocket of his overall jacket. He was going to put it under his pillow and wish that Sounder wasn't dead.

The wind had stopped blowing. This would have been a good hunting night, he thought. Far away, a single lantern was moving into the foothills. The boy was still crying. He had not forgotten the wood. Now he put out the lantern and hung it against the wall. He went to the woodpile, picked up two chunk-sticks, and went into the cabin.

The loneliness that was always in the cabin, except when his mother was singing or telling a story about the Lord, was heavier than ever now. It made the boy's tongue heavy. It pressed against his eyes, and they burned. It rolled against his ears. His head seemed to be squeezed inward, and it hurt. He noticed grease spots on the floor where the oak slab and the ham had fallen. He knew his mother had picked them up. His father would be cold, he thought, with that great rip in his overalls.

His mother sat by the stove. "You must eat," the woman said. The boy had been outside a long time. His mother had fed the other children, and they were already in bed. She did not take down her walnut basket to begin the slow filling of her apron with fat kernels. She did not sing or even

31

hum. "Child . . . child" she would say with long spaces between. Sometimes she would murmur to herself with her eyes closed. His little brother would murmur and be addled in his sleep tonight, the boy thought. He would set as long as his mother would let him. Maybe his mother would let him set and listen all night.

The boy listened for a yelp, a whine, a thump, thump, thump under the floor. There was no sound. His mother's rocker did not even move enough to squeak. One chunk-stick burning atop another in the stove rolled against the stove door with a slight thump. The boy started toward the cabin door.

"You know it was the stove," the mother said as she reached for the poker to push the wood back from the door.

"It sounded outside," the boy said as he pulled the door closed after him.

Soon he returned carrying the lantern. "I want to look more," he said. "I keep hearin' things." He lit the lantern from the stove as he had done before. His mother said nothing. He had thought she might say "Hang it back, child" as she often did when he wanted to go along the fencerows and hunt with Sounder after dark.

Outside, he murmured to himself, "That was

the stove, I reckon." He put the lantern on the ground and tried to see under the cabin. Nothing moved in the dim light. He wished the light would shine in Sounder's eyes and he would see them in the dark, but it didn't. Backing from under the porch on his hands and knees, he touched the lantern and tipped it over. He grabbed it by the wire rim that held the top of the globe and burned his hand. "Don't let it fall over; it'll explode" his father had said to him so many times when they hunted together. He sucked his burned fingers to draw out the fire. Sounder's pan was on the ground, and someone had stepped on it. The mean man who had kicked him with his big boot, the boy thought. He straightened it as best he could with his hurt fingers and put it on the porch.

He blew out the lantern and hung it by the possum sack. He stood on the porch and listened to the faraway. The lantern he had seen going into the foothills had disappeared. There were gravestones behind the meetin' house. Some were almost hidden in the brambles. If the deputy sheriff had turned around on the seat of the wagon and shot his father, the visiting preacher and somebody would bring him back and bury him behind the meetin' house, the boy thought. And if Sounder dies, I won't drag him over the hard earth. I'll carry him. I know I can carry him if I try hard enough, and I will bury him across the field, near the fencerow, under the big jack oak tree.

The boy picked up Sounder's bent tin pan and carried it into the cabin. The woman pushed back in her chair for a brief second in surprise and half opened her mouth. But, seeing the boy's face in the lamplight, she closed her mouth, and the rocker came slowly back to its standing position—her head tilted forward again, her eyes fixed on the boy's uneaten supper, still warming on the back of the stove.

In the corner of the room next to the dish cupboard, the boy filled Sounder's tin with cold ham-boiling from the possum kettle. "What's that for, child?" asked the mother slowly, as though she were sorry she had asked and would like to take it back.

"For if he comes out."

"You're hungry, child. Feed yourself."

The boy put Sounder's tin under the porch, closed the door, pushed the night latch, sat down behind the stove, and began to eat his supper.

III

IN THE MORNING the boy's mother did not cook any pork sausage for breakfast. The ham was on the tin-topped table, but she did not uncover it. Everybody had biscuits and milk gravy. There was still a faint smell of ham, but the boy missed the scent of sausage coming up to him as he stood warming himself. He had hurried out and called Sounder and looked under the house before he had finished buttoning his shirt, but his mother

35

had made him come in. She knew he would be crawling under the cabin, so she made him put on last year's worn-out overalls and a ragged jacket of his father's that came down to his knees. It wouldn't keep out much cold because it was full of holes.

The boy's mother put what was left of the pork sausage and the ham in a meal sack. When she had wrapped her walnut kernels in brown paper and tied them with string, she tied a scarf around her head and put on a heavy brown sweater that had pink flannel-outing patches on the elbows. She put the brown package in the basket she always carried when she went to the store. She put the meal sack over her shoulder.

"I'm taking the kernels to the store to sell them," she said to the boy. She did not say where she was going with the meal sack she had swung over her shoulder.

"Watch the fire, child," she said. "Don't go out of hollerin' distance and leave the young ones. Don't let them out in the cold.

"Warm some mush in the skillet for you all to eat at dinnertime. I'll be home before suppertime.

"Whatever you do, child, don't leave the children with a roaring fire and go lookin' for Sounder.

You ain't gonna find him this day. If a stranger comes, don't say nothin'."

The boy had nodded each time she spoke. He thought he would say "Yes" or "Don't worry, I will," but he didn't. He pushed the younger children back out of the cold and closed the door.

As his mother stepped off the porch and started for the road she began to hum softly to herself. It was a song the boy had heard her sing many nights in the cabin:

> *You gotta walk that lonesome valley,*
> *You gotta walk it by yourself,*
> *Ain't nobody else gonna walk it for you.*

The boy wanted to run after her. He watched as she became smaller and smaller, until the meal sack over her shoulder was just a white speck. The rest of her became a part of the brown road and the gray earth. When the white speck had faded into the earth, the boy looked up at the sky.

"No sun to thaw things out today," he said aloud to himself. His father always spoke aloud to the wind and the sky, and sometimes to the sun when he stood on the porch in the morning, especially when it rose out of the far lowland cottonwoods and pines like a great ball of fire. "Warmin' the cold bones" his father would say. And preparing for a hunt, his father would caution a full moon, hanging over the foothills, "Don't shine too bright, you'll make the creatures skittish." And Sounder too, settin' on his haunches, would speak to the moon in ghost-stirrin' tones of lonesome dog-talk.

People would be very mean to his mother today, the boy thought. He wondered if she would tell them that the ham had slid across the floor. If she told them, they might just throw it out and feed it to their dogs. They might let his mother keep it and bring it home again. They wouldn't let her keep the pork sausage, for it was wrapped in clean white paper and not cooked. They might push and pull his mother and put her in the back of a spring wagon and take her away too. She would spill the walnut kernels, and then she wouldn't be able to sell them to buy sowbelly and potatoes.

The boy had hoped the sun would shine. It would soften the frozen crust of earth and make it easier for him to dig a grave for Sounder—if he found Sounder. If Sounder was dead, he hoped no one would come along and see him carrying the grub hoe and shovel across the field to the big jack oak. They would ask what he was doing. If anybody passed while he was digging the grave, he would hide in the fencerow. If they saw him, they might run him off the land.

He felt like crying, but he didn't. Crying would only bother him. He would have his hands full of tools or be carrying Sounder's body. His nose would start dripping and be powerful troublesome because he wouldn't have a free hand to wipe it.

He took in an armload of wood and punched up the fire. "Don't open the stove door," he cautioned the younger children. "I have to go out some more." He went to his bed and took Sounder's ear from under the pillow. He would bury it with Sounder. He smelled his pillow. It still smelled clean and fresh. He put the ear in his pocket so the children wouldn't ask questions as he passed them on the way out. He smoothed his pillow. He was glad his mother washed his sheet and pillowcase every week, just like she did for the people who lived in the big houses with curtains on the windows. About twice a year his mother washed a lot of curtains. The clothesline was filled with them, and they were thin and light and ruffled and fluffy. It was more fun to rub your face against the curtains than on the clean sheets every Monday. The curtains, moving in the breeze, were like the sea's foam. The boy had never seen sea foam, but his mother had told him that when the Lord calmed the mighty Jordan for people to cross over, the water moved in little ripples like curtains in a breeze, and soft white foam made ruffles on top of the water.

The boy had never looked out of a window that had curtains on it. Whenever he passed houses with curtains on the windows, he remembered that if he put his face close against the curtains on the washline he could see through them. He thought there were always eyes, close against the curtains, looking out at him. He watched the windows out of the corner of his eye; he always felt scared until he had passed. Passing a cabin was different. In a cabin window there were just faces with real eyes looking out.

He could go out now, he thought. The wood in the stove had burned down some, and it would be safe. Besides, he would be close by for a while. Getting the body of Sounder from under the cabin wouldn't be easy. The younger children would bother him; they would ask a lot of questions like "Why is Sounder dead?" and "Will he stay dead?" and many more that he would not want to answer.

"When I'm out, don't be yellin' for me. I'll be through in a while," he said to the smallest child, who was looking out of the window, his chin barely high enough to rest on the sill.

There's no hurry, the boy thought. I have all day, and it's still early. And he looked out of the window too. "If you're inside you look out, and if you're outside you look in, but what looks both ways? That's a riddle; what's the answer?" He directed it to no child in particular. And no one answered. "What's the answer?" the boy repeated, and then he answered his own riddle. "The window is the answer; it looks both ways." None of the children paid any attention.

"I must go now," said the boy to his brother and sisters, "before it gets colder. The wind is starting up, so keep the door shut."

Sounder had not died in his favorite spot right behind the porch steps where he had a hole dug out and where the boy's father had put two coffee sacks for a pallet. His mother had said, "Sounder will crawl to the darkest, farthest part of the cabin." That's why she had made the boy put on his ragged clothes.

The boy could not see all the way under the cabin. At one time rats had lived there, and they had pushed up the earth in some places so that it almost touched the beams. They did this so they could gnaw through the floor from below.

He hurt his head and shoulders on nails sticking down from above as he crawled. He hurt his knees and elbows on broken glass, rusty sardine cans, and broken pieces of crockery and dishes. The dry dust got in his mouth and tasted like lime and grease. Under the cabin it smelled stale and dead, like old carcasses and snakes. The boy was glad it was winter because in summer there might have been dry-land moccasins and copperheads under the cabin. He crawled from front to back, looking along the spaces between the beams.

Sounder was not to be seen. The boy would have to go back and forth. Maybe Sounder had pushed with his hind feet and dug a hole into which he had settled. The threadbare knees of last year's overalls opened up, and his bare knees scraped the soil. His father's long jacket caught under his knees as he crawled and jerked his face down into the dust. Cobwebs drooped over his face and mouth. His mouth was so dry with dust that he could not spit them out.

He crawled over every spot under the cabin, but Sounder's body was not there. The boy felt in his pocket. He had lost Sounder's ear under the cabin. It made no difference. It could be buried there.

But where was Sounder's body? he wondered.

Perhaps the injuries in the side of his head and shoulder were only skin wounds. They looked so terrible, but maybe they were not bad after all. Perhaps Sounder had limped down the road, the way the wagon had taken his master, and died. Perhaps he had only been knocked senseless and that was why he zigzagged so crazily, running for the cabin.

No wild creature could have carried the dead body away. Foxes could carry off dead squirrels and possums. But no animal was big enough to drag Sounder's body away. Maybe the boy, looking under the cabin with the lantern, had caused Sounder to crawl out the other side and die in the brown stalk land.

The boy was crying now. Not that there was any new or sudden sorrow. There just seemed to be nothing else to fill up the vast lostness of the moment. His nose began to run and itch. The tears ran down through the cobwebs and dust that covered his face, making little rivulets. The boy rubbed his eyes with his dirty hands and mixed dust with tears. His eyes began to smart.

He followed the road the way the wagon had taken his father as far as he dared leave the fire and the children in the cabin, still in hollering distance. There was no sign of Sounder's body.

44

He spiraled the brown stalk land in ever-widening circles, searching the fencerows as he went. Under the jack oaks and the cottonwoods there was nothing. In the matted Scotch-broom tangle he visualized the great tan body as he carefully picked each step. But the dog was not there.

IV

AFTER THE BOY had fed the children and eaten something himself, he sat down by the warm stove and looked out of the window. There was nothing else to do. Now and then a cloud would cross the sun that had finally burned its way out of the gray. The boy watched the cloud shadows roll over the fields and pass over the cabin. They darkened the window as they passed.

He carried in wood for the night before the sun

began to weaken. Then he looked out of the window again to where his mother would appear. Finally he saw a speck moving on the road. He watched it grow.

"She's coming," he said to the younger children, and they crowded around him and pushed their faces against the window. "She's been gone long enough to walk to town and more," he added.

"What will she bring?" one of the children asked.

"She'll bring nothin', but maybe things to eat. She won't bring no stick candy. Don't ask her for none. Don't ask her nothin'."

Several times during the day the boy had said to himself, "Maybe they'll let him come home if she takes back the stuff. Some people might, but some won't." But his father was not with her.

"I gave the stuff back," she said when she got to the cabin.

The boy's throat hurt with a great lump, and when he swallowed, it would hurt more. If his father had come, it would have been easy. Together they could have found Sounder's body and buried him.

When the boy's mother heard that he had not found Sounder under the cabin, she stood in the doorway and thought for a long time. If one of the children had stood in the door that long, she would have said "Go in or out, child."

"Creatures like to die under somethin'," she said at last, "and there ain't nothin' else close to crawl under. He wasn't hit in his vitals, I reckon. He's got a flesh wound. He's gone into the woods to draw out the poison with oak-leaf acid."

Now she shut the door and put her basket on the tin-topped table. "Poke up the fire," she said to the boy. "Oak leaves has strong acid that toughens the skin, just like the oak bark that they use to tan leather in the tannery. The creature beds down with the wound against a heap of oak leaves. The leaves make a poultice that draws out the poison and heals the wound with a hard brown scab. That's why creatures head for the swampland around the big water when the mange hits. Wet leaves heals better."

"Sounder's blood would wettin the leaves," the boy said after he had stood a long time with the poker in his hand. His eyes were fixed on the open stove door, watching the yellow flame change shape and turn to blue and red.

"Sounder was jumping at the wagon and hard to hit," the boy's mother said. "I think maybe he was hit a glancing shot that tore off the hide on his head and shoulder. If he was, he's gone to the jack-oak woods to heal himself. The Lord shows

48

His creatures how to do. If he ain't dead now, he'll come limpin' home, powerful hungry, in time."

"Tomorrow or the day after?" the boy asked.

"Longer, maybe four days, or more like seven. But don't be all hope, child. If he had deep head wounds, he might be addled crazy and not know where he wandered off to die."

The boy's mother had brought home the empty meal sack. In her basket she had some fat meat, potatoes, and a small bottle of vanilla flavoring, which she had bought with the money she got for her walnut kernels. From the bottom of the basket she took the folded brown paper bag into which she poured each night's pickin's and put it on the shelf. She also brought home an empty cardboard box which the storekeeper had given her. She didn't say where she had been, besides the store, or what had happened. The boy could see that her eyes were filled with hurt and said nothing. The younger children remembered not to ask anything except, looking in the empty box, one said, "Nothin' in here?"

"I'm gonna use it to put a cake in," the mother said.

"Better go out and crack nuts for the night's pickin' before dark," she said to the boy.

The boy scooped up a tin pail of nuts from the

big box under the stove and went out to the flat cracking stone. With his knees still sore from crawling under the cabin, he hesitated a long time before he knelt on the frozen earth. Standing, he looked one way and then another, tracing the fencerows that had more oaks than other trees, the far lowland woods and the foothills. "I'll go there first tomorrow," he said to himself as he faced the foothills. "There's big patches of oak trees there. And whenever Sounder was given his head, he picked the hills for huntin'."

When night came, his mother hummed and picked kernels. She did not tell a story. The boy wanted to ask who carried in wood to keep the people in jail warm. He knew they had big stoves in big jails. Once his mother had told him a story about three people named Shadrach, Meshach, and Abed-nego who were in jail. Some mean governor or sheriff got mad and had them thrown right into the jail stove, big as a furnace, but the Lord blew out the fire and cooled the big stove in a second. And when the jail keeper opened the stove door, there stood Shadrach, Meshach, and Abed-nego singing:

> Cool water, cool water;
> The Lord's got green pastures and cool water.

"Tell me about Joseph in the jail and the stone

quarry in Egypt and chiselin' out rocks to make ole Pharaoh's gravestone," the boy asked. But his mother went on humming, and the boy went back to his thinking.

No stove could be that big, he thought. He watched the red coals through the open draft in the stove door brighten each time the wind blew loud enough to make a low whistling noise in the stovepipe. A burning chunk-stick fell against the inside of the stove, but the boy did not try to convince himself that it might be the thump of Sounder scratching fleas underneath the floor. He was thinking of tomorrow.

Tomorrow he would go into the woods and look for Sounder. "The wind whistlin' in the pipe is bothersome," he said. He hated the cold wind. It blew through his clothes and chilled his body inside and made him shiver. He hoped the wind would not be blowing in the woods tomorrow. The wind made the woods noisy. The boy liked the woods when they were quiet. He understood quiet. He could hear things in the quiet. But quiet was better in the woods than it was in the cabin. He didn't hear things in cabin quiet. Cabin quiet was long and sad.

"Turn the pipe-damper a little and the whistlin' will stop," his mother said at last.

The next day he walked the great woodlands,

calling Sounder's name. The wind blew through his clothes and chilled him inside. When he got home after dark, his clothes were torn. His throat hurt with a great lump choking him. His mother fed him and said, "Child, child, you must not go into the woods again. Sounder might come home again. But you must learn to lose, child. The Lord teaches the old to lose. The young don't know how to learn it. Some people is born to keep. Some is born to lose. We was born to lose, I reckon. But Sounder might come back."

But weeks went by, and Sounder did not come back.

*   *   *

One night the boy learned why his mother had brought home the bottle of vanilla flavoring. Now it was Christmas and she was making a cake. When the four layers were spread out on the tin-topped table and she began to ice them, the boy noticed that she put three together in a large cake and made a small one of the leftover layer.

"Why we having two cakes?" the boy asked. But she was humming to herself and did not answer him. When she had finished, she put the small cake on the top shelf of the dish cupboard. The big one she put in the cardboard box she had brought from the store.

The sweet smell of baking and vanilla had drawn the smaller children from the stove to the edge of the table. The woman reached over or walked around them as she worked. "I'm done," she finally said. "You can lick the pans."

The boy had not moved from his chair by the stove. Today he had searched the oak clumps along the far fencerows for Sounder. He never got the sweet pan till last, anyway. It always went from youngest to oldest, and there was never much left when his turn came.

"You're tired and worried poorly," his mother said. And she handed him the icing pan.

In the morning the woman told the boy that she wanted him to walk to town, to the jail behind the courthouse, and take the cake to his father. "It's a troublesome trip," she said. "But they won't let women in the jail. So you must go." She tied a string around the cardboard box and said, "Carry it flat if your hands don't get too cold. Then it'll look mighty pretty when you fetch it to him." She stood at the edge of the porch until he was far enough away not to be able to look back and see her crying, then called to him,

"Whatever you do, child, act perkish and don't grieve your father."

On the road, the boy felt afraid. He had been to the town at Christmastime before. Not on Christmas Day, but a few days before, to help his father carry mistletoe and bunches of bittersweet berries that his father sold by the wall in front of the courthouse or on the corner by the bank. And sometimes, when it was getting late and they still had trimmings to sell, his father would go to the back door of houses along the street and say "Ma'am, would you need some trimmin's?" and hold up the biggest sprig of mistletoe left in his grain sack. They usually sold most of the mistletoe, the boy remembered, but bunches of bittersweet that the boy had carried all day were always left over to be thrown in a fence corner on the way home. "Ain't no good for nothin' now" his father would say.

From early fall until gathering time, the father and boy kept their eyes peered for the golden-green clumps with white berries that grew high up in the forks of water elm and sycamore trees. Bittersweet was easy. "Pull down one vine and trim it, and you've got as much as a man can carry" his father always said. "But it takes a heap of fearful climbin' for mistletoe." They had al-

54

ready started gathering, and half a grain sack of mistletoe was still hanging against the side of the cabin. "If she hadn't had such a big load, she might have taken it," the boy said to himself.

The boy's fearful feeling increased as he got nearer town. There were big houses and behind the curtained windows there were eyes looking out at him. There would be more people now, and somebody might say "What you got in that box, boy?" or "Where you goin', boy?"

Church bells were ringing in the town. It was Christmas, and some people went to church on Christmas. In town the people he saw were laughing and talking. No one noticed him and he was glad. He looked at the store windows out of the corner of his eye. They were silvery and gold and green and red and sparkling. They were filled with toys and beautiful things. With the Christmas money from peddling, his father had bought what toys he could for the boy and his little brother and sisters. They had worn-out toys too. People in the big houses where his mother worked had given them to her to bring home.

He always wished they would give his mother an old book. He was sure he could learn to read if he had a book. He could read some of the town signs and the store signs. He could read price figures. He wanted to stop and stand and look straight at the windows, but he was afraid. A policeman would come after him. Perhaps the people had offered his mother old books, but she had said "No use, nobody can read in our cabin." Perhaps the people knew she couldn't read and thought her feelings would be hurt if they offered her the books their children had used up and worn out. The boy had heard once that some people had so many books they only read each book once. But the boy was sure there were not that many books in the world.

It was cold, but there were a few people standing or sitting along the wall in front of the courthouse. Winter or summer, there were always people there. The boy wondered if they knew it was Christmas. They didn't look happy like some of the people he had seen. He knew they were looking at him, so he hurried quickly past and around the corner to the back of the courthouse. The front of the courthouse was red brick with great white marble steps going up to a wide door. But the back was gray cement and three floors high, with iron bars over all the windows.

The only door that led into the jail had a small square of glass at about the height of a man, and there were iron bars over the glass. The boy was not tall enough to see through the glass. He

clutched the box close to him. He felt that something was about to burst through the door. In the middle of the door there was a great iron knocker. The boy knew he had to knock at the door; he wished he could be back in the great woods. He could hear voices inside the windows with the iron bars. Somewhere a voice was singing "God's gonna trouble the water." From one of the windows there came the sound of laughter. Now and then a door slammed with the deep clash of iron on iron. There was a rattle of tin pans. The boy felt very lonely. The town was as lonely as the cabin, he thought.

A large red-faced man opened the door and said, "You'll have to wait. It ain't visitin' hours yet. Who do you want to see? You'll have to wait." And he slammed the door before the boy could speak.

It was cold on the gray side of the building, so the boy went to the corner near the wall where the people and visitors stood or sat. The sun was shining there. The boy had forgotten it was still Christmas, the waiting seemed so long. A drunk man staggered along the street in front of the courthouse wall, saying "Merry Christmas" to everyone. He said "Merry Christmas" to the boy, and he smiled at the boy too.

Finally the great clock on the roof of the courthouse struck twelve. It frightened the boy because it seemed to shake the town. Now the red-faced man opened the door and let several people in. Inside, the man lined everybody up and felt their clothes and pockets. He jerked the cardboard box from the boy and tore off the top. The boy could hear iron doors opening and closing. Long hallways, with iron bars from floor to ceiling, ran from the door into the dim center of the building. The man with the red face squeezed the cake in his hands and broke it into four pieces. "This could have a steel file or hacksaw blade in it," he said. Then he swore and threw the pieces back in the box. The boy had been very hungry. Now he was not hungry. He was afraid. The man shoved the box into the boy's hands and swore again. Part of the cake fell to the floor; it was only a box of crumbs now. The man swore again and made the boy pick up the crumbs from the floor.

The boy hated the man with the red face with the same total but helpless hatred he had felt when he saw his father chained, when he saw Sounder shot. He had thought how he would like to chain the deputy sheriff behind his own wagon and then scare the horse so that it would run faster than the cruel man could. The deputy would fall and bounce and drag on the frozen road. His fine leather jacket would be torn more than he had torn his father's overalls. He would yell and curse, and that would make the horse go faster. And the boy would just watch, not trying to stop the wagon. . . .

The boy would like to see the big red-faced man crumpled on the floor with the crumbs. Besides the red face, the boy had noticed the fat, bulging neck that folded down over the man's collar and pushed up in wrinkled circles under his chin. The bull neck of the man reminded the boy of the bull he had seen die in the cattle chute at the big house where his father worked. The horse doctor had been trying to vaccinate the bull in the neck, but the rope through the ring in the bull's nose didn't keep the bull from tossing his head from side to side, knocking the horse doctor against the side of the chute. Then the horse doctor had gotten mad and said, "Get a chain. I'll make him stand still."

When the chain was snapped around the bull's neck, the farm hands pulled it over the crossbar of the chute posts and hooked it. But when the horse doctor stuck the bull in the neck, he lunged backward, set his front feet with his whole weight against the chain, and choked himself to death before one of the farm hands could jab him with a pitchfork and make him slacken the chain. The legs of the bull folded under him and the chain

60

buried itself in the fat of his neck. When the farm hands finally got the chain unhooked from the crossbar, the bull's head fell in the dirt, and blood oozed out of its mouth and nostrils. . . .

The bull-necked man would sag to his knees, the boy thought, and crumple into a heap on the floor. Just the way the bull did, the boy thought, and blood would ooze out of his mouth and nose.

"Get up," the red-faced man said, "you wanta take all day?" The boy stood up. He felt weak and his knees shook, but there were no more tears in his eyes.

The red-faced man took a big iron key on a ring as big around as the boy's head and unlocked one of the iron gates. He pushed the boy in and said, "Fourth door down." Passing the three doors, the boy could feel eyes following him. He saw men, some sitting on cots, some standing behind the iron gates with their hands on the bars, looking at him. Each step echoed against the iron ceiling and made him sound like a giant walking. Far down the long iron-grated corridor a sad voice was singing:

> Far away on Judah's plains
> The shepherds watched their sheep.

The boy's father stood with his hands on the bars. He did not have his hands and feet chained together. Seeing the hands that could handle a hot pot lid without a pot rag, open the stove door without using a poker, or skin a possum by holding the hind legs of the carcass with one hand and the hide with the other and just pulling, the boy knew his father could have choked the cruel man with the bull neck.

The father looked at the boy and said, "Child." On the way, the boy had thought about what he would say to his father. He had practiced talking about his mother selling kernels at the store and buying the cake makings, his little brother and sisters being all right, no strangers coming past, not finding Sounder's body. And he was going to ask his father where Sounder came to him along the road when he wasn't more'n a pup. He practiced saying them all over and over to get the quiver and the quiet spells out of his voice because his mother had said, "Whatever you do, child, act perkish and don't grieve your father."

But the boy was full of mixed hate and pity now, and it addled him. There was an opening in the bars with a flat, iron shelf attached on the inside. The boy had left the lid of the box on the floor. Now he pushed the box through the opening and said, "This was a cake, before—" But he couldn't finish. An awful quiet spell destroyed all his practice.

"Sounder might not be dead," the boy said. He knew his father was grieved, for he swallowed hard and the quiet spells came to him too.

"I'll be back 'fore long," said his father.

From somewhere down the corridor there came a loud belly laugh, and a loud voice called out, "Listen to the man talk."

"Tell her not to grieve." His father was almost whispering now.

"Sounder didn't die under the cabin." But the boy couldn't keep the quivering out of his voice.

"Tell her not to send you no more." The quiet spells were getting longer. The man stopped looking through the bars at the boy and looked down at the cake.

"If he wasn't shot in his vitals," the boy said, "he might get healed in the woods." Then there was a long quiet spell that was split in the middle by the loud clank of an iron door banging shut.

"Tell her I'll send word with the visitin' preacher."

The big red-faced man with the bull neck opened the corridor door and yelled, "Visitin' over." The boy felt numb and cold, like he had felt standing outside the jail door. He choked up. He had grieved his father. He hated the red-faced man, so he wouldn't cry until he got outside.

"Come on, boy," the man yelled, swinging the big key ring.

"Go, child," the father said. "Hurry, child."

The boy was the last person through the big iron door. The bull-necked man pushed him and said, "Git, boy, or next time you won't get in."

V

THE BOY MOVED quickly around the corner and out of sight of the iron door and the gray cement walls of the jail. At the wall in front of the courthouse he stood for a while and looked back. When he had come, he was afraid, but he felt good in one way because he would see his father. He was bringing him a cake for Christmas. And he wasn't going to let his father know he was grieved. So his father *wouldn't* be grieved.

Now the sun had lost its strength. There were only a few people loafing around the courthouse wall, so the boy sat for a spell. He felt numb and tired. What would he say to his mother? He would tell her that the jailer was mean to visitors but didn't say nothing to the people in jail. He wouldn't tell her about the cake. When he told her his father had said she shouldn't send him again, that he would send word by the visiting preacher, she would say "You grieved him, child. I told you to be perk so you wouldn't grieve him."

Nobody came near where the boy sat or passed on the street in front of the wall. He had forgotten the most important thing, he thought. He hadn't asked his father where Sounder had come to him on the road when he wasn't more'n a pup. That didn't make any difference.

But along the road on the way to the jail, before the bull-necked man had ruined everything, the boy had thought his father would begin to think and say "If a stray ever follard you and it wasn't near a house, likely somebody's dropped it. So you could fetch it home and keep it for a dog."

"Wouldn't do no good now," the boy murmured to himself. Even if he found a stray on the way home, his mother would say "I'm afraid, child.

Don't bring it in the cabin. If it's still here when mornin' comes, you take it down the road and scold it and run so it won't foller you no more. If somebody come lookin', you'd be in awful trouble."

A great part of the way home the boy walked in darkness. In the big houses he saw beautiful lights and candles in the windows. Several times dogs rushed to the front gates and barked as he passed. But no stray pup came to him along the lonely, empty stretches of road. In the dark he thought of the bull-necked man crumpled on the floor in the cake crumbs, like the strangled bull in the cattle chute, and he walked faster. At one big house the mailbox by the road had a lighted lantern hanging on it. The boy walked on the far side of the road so he wouldn't show in the light. "People hangs 'em out when company is comin' at night," the boy's father had once told him.

When court was over, they would take his father to a road camp or a quarry or a state farm. Would his father send word with the visiting preacher where he had gone? Would they take his father away to the chain gang for a year or two years before he could tell the visiting preacher? How would the boy find him then? If he lived closer to the town, he could watch each day, and when they took his father away in the wagons where convicts were penned up in huge wooden crates, he could follow.

The younger children were already in bed when the boy got home. He was glad, for they would have asked a lot of questions that might make his mother feel bad, questions like "Is everybody chained up in jail? How long do people stay in jail at one time?"

The boy's mother did not ask hurtful questions. She asked if the boy got in all right and if it was warm in the jail. The boy told her that the jailer was mean to visitors but that he didn't say nothing to the people in jail. He told her he heard some people singing in the jail.

"Sounder ain't come home?" the boy said to his mother after he had talked about the jail. He had looked under the porch and called before he came into the cabin.

Now he went out, calling and looking around the whole cabin. He started to light the lantern to look more, but his mother said, "Hang it back, child. Ain't no use to fret yourself. Eat your supper, you must be famished."

"He said not to come no more," the boy finally said to his mother when he had finished his supper. "He said he'll send word by the visitin' preacher." He poked up the fire and waited for his mother to ask him if he had been perk and didn't grieve his father, but she didn't. He warmed himself and watched a patch of red glow the size of his hand at the bottom of the stove. He could see the red-faced man lying on the jail floor with blood oozing out of the corners of his mouth. After a long quiet spell the rocker began to squeak, and it made the boy jump, but his mother didn't notice. She began to rock as she picked out walnut kernels. She hummed for a while, and then she began to sing like she was almost whispering for no one to hear but herself:

> *You've gotta walk that lonesome valley,*
> *You've gotta walk it by yourself,*
> *Ain't nobody else gonna walk it for you ...*

In bed, the pressure of the bed slats through the straw tick felt good against the boy's body. His pillow smelled fresh, and it was smooth and soft. He was tired, but he lay awake for a long time. He thought of the store windows full of so many things. He thought of the beautiful candles in windows. He dreamed his father's hands were chained against the prison bars and he was still standing there with his head down. He dreamed that a wonderful man had come up to him as he was trying to read the store signs aloud and had said, "Child, you want to learn, don't you?"

In the morning the boy lay listening to his

mother as she opened and closed the stove door. He heard the damper squeak in the stovepipe as she adjusted it. She was singing softly to herself. Then the boy thought he heard another familiar sound, a faint whine on the cabin porch. He listened. No, it couldn't be. Sounder always scratched before he whined, and the scratching was always louder than the whine. Besides, it was now almost two months later, and the boy's mother had said he might be back in a week. No, he was not dreaming. He heard it again. He had been sleeping in his shirt to keep warm, so he only had to pull on his overalls as he went. His mother had stopped singing and was listening.

There on the cabin porch, on three legs, stood the living skeleton of what had been a mighty coon hound. The tail began to wag, and the hide made little ripples back and forth over the ribs. One side of the head and shoulders was reddish brown and hairless; the acid of the oak leaves had tanned the surface of the wound the color of leather. One front foot dangled above the floor. The stub of an ear stuck out on one side, and there was no eye on that side, only a dark socket with a splinter of bone showing above it. The dog raised his good ear and whined. His one eye looked up at the lantern and the possum sack

70

where they hung against the wall. The eye looked past the boy and his mother. Where was his master? "Poor creature. Poor creature," said the mother and turned away to get him food. The boy felt sick and wanted to cry, but he touched Sounder on the good side of his head. The tail wagged faster, and he licked the boy's hand.

The shattered shoulder never grew together enough to carry weight, so the great hunter with the single eye, his head held to one side so he could see, never hopped much farther from the cabin than the spot in the road where he had tried to jump on the wagon with his master. Whether he lay in the sun on the cabin porch or by the side of the road, the one eye was always turned in the direction his master had gone.

The boy got used to the way the great dog looked. The stub of ear didn't bother him, and the one eye that looked up at him was warm and questioning. But why couldn't he bark? "He wasn't hit in the neck" the boy would say to his mother. "He eats all right, his throat ain't scarred." But day after day when the boy snapped his fingers and said "Sounder, good Sounder," no excited bark burst from the great throat. When something moved at night, the whine was louder, but it was still just a whine.

Before Sounder was shot, the boy's mother always said "Get the pan, child" or "Feed your dog, child." Now she sometimes got the pan herself and took food out to Sounder. The boy noticed that sometimes his mother would stop singing when she put the food pan down at the edge of the porch. Sometimes she would stand and look at the hunting lantern and possum sack where they hung, unused, against the cabin wall. . . .

*   *   *

The town and the jail seemed to become more remote and the distance greater as each day passed. If his father hadn't said "Don't come again," it wouldn't seem so far, the boy thought. Uncertainty made the days of waiting longer too.

The boy waited for the visiting preacher to come and bring word of his father. He thought the people for whom his mother washed the soft curtains could certainly write and would write a letter for his mother. But would someone in the jail read it for his father? Perhaps none of the people in jail could read, and the big man with the red face would just tear it up and swear. The visiting preacher might write a letter for the boy's father. But how would it get to the cabin since no mailman passed and there was no mailbox like the boy had seen on the wider road nearer the town?

The boy wanted to go to the town to find out what had happened to his father. His mother always said "Wait, child, wait." When his mother returned laundry to the big houses, she asked the people to read her the court news from their newspapers. One night she came home with word of the boy's father; it had been read to her from the court news. When the younger children had gone to bed, she said to the boy, "Court's over." And then there was one of those long quiet spells that always made the boy feel numb and weak.

"You won't have to fret for a while about seein' him in jail. He's gone to hard labor."

"For how long?" the boy asked.

"It won't be as long as it might. Folks has always said he could do two men's work in a day. He'll get time off for hard work and good behavior. The court news had about good behavior in it. The judge said it."

"Where's he gonna be at?" the boy asked after he had swallowed the great lump that filled up his throat and choked him.

"Didn't say. The people that has the paper says

74

it don't ever say wher' they gonna be at. But it's the county or the state. Ain't never outside the state, the people says."

"He'll send word," the boy said.

VI

NOW THE CABIN was even quieter than it had been before loneliness put its stamp on everything. Sounder rolled his one eye in lonely dreaming. The boy's mother had longer periods of just humming without drifting into soft singing. The boy helped her stretch longer clotheslines from the cabin to the cottonwood trees at the edge of the fields. In the spring the boy went to the fields to work. He was younger than the other workers.

He was afraid and lonely. He heard them talking quietly about his father. He went to do yard work at the big houses where he had gathered weeds behind his father. "How old are you?" a man asked once when he was paying the boy his wages. "You're a hard worker for your age."

The boy did not remember his age. He knew he had lived a long, long time.

And the long days and months and seasons built a powerful restlessness into the boy. "Don't fret" his mother would say when he first began to talk of going to find his father. "Time's passin'. Won't be much longer now."

To the end of the county might be a far journey, and out of the county would be a far, far journey, but I'll go, the boy thought.

"Why are you so feared for me to go?" he would ask, for now he was old enough to argue with his mother. "In Bible stories everybody's always goin' on a long journey. Abraham goes on a long journey. Jacob goes into a strange land where his uncle lives, and he don't know where he lives, but he finds him easy. Joseph goes on the longest journey of all and has more troubles, but the Lord watches over him. And in Bible-story journeys, ain't no journey hopeless. Everybody finds what they suppose to find."

The state had many road camps which moved from place to place. There were also prison farms and stone quarries. Usually the boy would go searching in autumn when work in the fields was finished. One year he heard "Yes, the man you speak of was here, but I heard he was moved to the quarry in Gilmer County." One year it had been "Yes, he was in the quarry, but he was sick in the winter and was moved to the bean farm in Bartow County." More often a guard would chase him away from the gate or from standing near the high fence with the barbed wire along the top of it. And the guard would laugh and say "I don't know no names; I only know numbers. Besides, you can't visit here, you can only visit in jail." Another would sneer "You wouldn't know your old man if you saw him, he's been gone so long. You sure you know who your pa is, kid?"

The men in striped convict suits, riding in the mule-drawn wagons with big wooden frames resembling large pig crates, yelled as they rode past the watching boy, "Hey, boy, looking for your big brother? What you doing, kid, seeing how you gonna like it when you grow up?" And still the boy would look through the slats of the crate for a familiar face. He would watch men walking in line, dragging chains on their feet, to see if he

78

could recognize his father's step as he had known it along the road, coming from the fields to the cabin. Once he listened outside the gate on a Sunday afternoon and heard a preacher telling about the Lord loosening the chains of Peter when he had been thrown into prison. Once he stood at the guardhouse door of a quarry, and some ladies dressed in warm heavy coats and boots came and sang Christmas songs.

In his wandering the boy learned that the words men use most are "Get!" "Get out!" and "Keep moving!" Sometimes he followed the roads from one town to another, but if he could, he would follow railroad tracks. On the roads there were people, and they frightened the boy. The railroads usually ran through the flat silent countryside where the boy could walk alone with his terrifying thoughts. He learned that railroad stations, post offices, courthouses, and churches were places to escape from the cold for a few hours in the late night.

His journeys in search of his father accomplished one wonderful thing. In the towns he found that people threw newspapers and magazines into trash barrels, so he could always find something with which to practice his reading. When he was tired, or when he waited at some high wire gate, hoping his father would pass in the line, he would read the big-lettered words first and then practice the small-lettered words.

In his lonely journeying, the boy had learned to tell himself the stories his mother had told him at night in the cabin. He liked the way they always ended with the right thing happening. And people in stories were never feared of anything. Sometimes he tried to put together things he had read in the newspapers he found and make new stories. But the ends never came out right, and they made him more afraid. The people he tried to put in stories from the papers always seemed like strangers. Some story people he wouldn't be afraid of if he met them on the road. He thought he liked the David and Joseph stories best of all. "Why you want 'em told over'n over?" his mother had asked so many times. Now, alone on a bed of pine needles, he remembered that he could never answer his mother. He would just wait, and if his mother wasn't sad, with her lips stretched thin, she would stop humming and tell about David the boy, or King David. If she felt good and started long enough before bedtime, he would hear about Joseph the slave-boy, Joseph in prison, Joseph the dreamer, and Joseph the Big Man in Egypt. And when she had finished all about Joseph, she would say "Ain't no earthly power can make a story end as pretty as Joseph's; 'twas the Lord."

The boy listened to the wind passing through the tops of the tall pines; he thought they moved like giant brooms sweeping the sky. The moonlight raced down through the broken spaces of swaying trees and sent bright shafts of light along the ground and over him. The voice of the wind in the pines reminded him of one of the stories his mother had told him about King David. The Lord had said to David that when he heard the wind moving in the tops of the cedar trees, he would know that the Lord was fighting on his side and he would win. When David moved his army around into the hills to attack his enemy, he heard the mighty roar of the wind moving in the tops of the trees, and he cried out to his men that the Lord was moving above them into battle.

The boy listened to the wind. He could hear the mighty roaring. He thought he heard the voice of David and the tramping of many feet. He wasn't afraid with David near. He thought he saw a lantern moving far off in the woods, and as he fell asleep he thought he heard the deep, ringing voice of Sounder rising out of his great throat, riding the mist of the lowlands.

VII

WHEN THE BOY came home after each long trip in search of his father, the crippled coon hound would hobble far down the road to meet him, wag his tail, stand on his hind legs, and paw the boy with his good front paw. But never a sound beyond a deep whine came from him. The bits of news he might bring home his mother received in silence. Someone had heard that his father was moved. Someone had been in the same work gang with his father for four months last summer on the Walker county road. When she had heard all he had heard, she would say "There's patience, child, and waitin' that's got to be."

Word drifted back that there had been a terrible dynamite blast in one of the quarries that had killed twelve convicts and wounded several others. His mother had had the people read her the story from their newspapers when she carried the laundry. None of the prisoners killed was the boy's father.

The months and seasons of searching dragged into years. The boy helped his mother carry more and more baskets of laundry to and from the big houses; the clotheslines grew longer and longer. The other children, except for the littlest, could fetch and tote too, but they didn't like to go by themselves.

"Time is passing" the woman would say. "I wish you wouldn't go lookin', child." But when one of the field hands had heard something or when somebody said that a road camp was moving, she would wrap a piece of bread and meat for the boy to eat on the way and say nothing. Looking back from far down the road, the boy would see her watching at the edge of the porch. She seemed to understand the compulsion that started him on each long, fruitless journey with new hope.

Once the boy waited outside the tall wire fence of a road camp. Some convicts were whitewashing stones along the edge of a pathway that came toward the gate near where he stood. One might be his father, he thought. He could not tell until they got closer, for they crawled on their hands and knees as they bent over the stones. He leaned against the fence and hooked his fingers through the wire. If none of them was his father, they might know something anyway, he thought. He wished they would stand up and walk from one stone to the next. Then he would know his father easily by his walk. He could still remember the sound of his footsteps approaching the cabin after dark, the easy roll of the never-hurrying step that was the same when he went to work in the morning and when he came home from the long day in the fields. The boy had even been able to tell his father's walk by the swing of the lantern at his side. But none of the men whitewashing the round rocks that lined the path stood up and walked. They crawled the few feet from stone to stone, and crawling, they all looked the same.

Suddenly something crashed against the fence in front of the boy's face. A jagged piece of iron tore open the skin and crushed the fingers of one of his hands against the fence. Lost in thought and watching the convicts, the boy had not seen the guard, who had been sitting under a tree with a shotgun across his knees, get up and come to a toolbox filled with picks and crowbars which stood near the fence.

The piece of iron lay on the inside of the fence at the boy's feet. Drops of blood from his fingers dripped down the fence from wire to wire and fell on the ground. The boy pulled his fingers away from the wire mesh and began to suck on them to stop the throbbing. Tears ran down over his face and mixed with the blood on his hand. Little rivulets of blood and water ran down his arm and dropped off the end of his elbow.

The guard was swaying back and forth with laughter. His gun lay on the lid of the open toolbox. His arms swung in apelike gyrations of glee, and he held another piece of iron in one hand and his cap in the other. A white strip of forehead, where his uniform cap kept off the sun, shone between his brown hair and his sunburned face. His laughter had burst the button from his tieless shirt collar, and a white strip outlined his gaunt neck. For a second he reminded the boy of a garden scarecrow blowing in the wind, body and head of brown burlap stuffed with straw, the head tied on with a white rag just like the white band around the guard's neck, the head tilting from side to side, inviting a well-placed stone to send it bouncing along a bean row.

The men whitewashing the rocks made no sounds. No one among them suddenly raised himself to the height of a man almost as tall as a cabin porch post.

"He ain't there," the boy murmured to himself. If he was, the boy knew, by now he would be holding the scarecrow of a man in the air with one hand clamped all the way around the white strip on the skinny neck, the way he had seen Sounder clamp his great jaws on a weasel once, with the head stuck out one side of the jaws and the body the other. And the man would wheeze and squirm like the weasel had. His legs would paw the air in circles like his hands, then he would go limp, and the boy's father would loosen his grip, and the man in the brown uniform would fall in a heap, like when somebody untied the white rag that held the scarecrow to the stake. And the heap would roll down the slope and lodge against the fence, like the scarecrow rolled along a bean row until it caught in the brambles at the edge of the garden.

Feeling defeat in the midst of his glee because the boy had not run but stood still and defiant, sucking the blood from his bruised fingers, the guard stopped laughing and yelled at him, "That'll show you, boy! Git! And git fast!" The boy turned and, without looking back, began to walk slowly away. The guard began to laugh again and threw the scrap of iron over the fence. It landed a few feet from the boy. He looked at the iron and he looked at the man. The white spot between his hair and his eyes was the spot. The iron would split it open with a wide gash, and blood would darken the white spot and make it the color of the man's sunburned face. And the stone that David slung struck Goliath on his forehead; the stone sank into his forehead, and he fell on his face on the ground, the boy thought. But he left the iron on the ground.

Still sucking his fingers, the boy looked once more at the men whitewashing the stones. They were almost at the gate. He didn't need to wait and ask. His father was not crawling among them.

*   *   *

Later that day, passing along a street in a strange and lonely town, he saw a man dump a box of trash into a barrel. He noticed that a large brown-backed book went in with the trash. He waited until the man went back into the building and then took the book from the barrel. It was a book of stories about what people think. There were titles such as Cruelty, Excellent Men, Education, Cripples, Justice, and many others. The boy sat down, leaned back against the barrel, and began to read from the story called Cruelty.

> I have often heard it said that cowardice is the mother of cruelty, and I have found by experience that malicious and inhuman animosity and fierceness are usually accompanied by weakness. Wolves and filthy bears, and all the baser beasts, fall upon the dying.

The boy was trying to read aloud, for he could understand better if he heard the words. But now he stopped. He did not understand what it said; the words were too new and strange. He was sad. He thought books would have words like the ones he had learned to read in the store signs, words like his mother used when she told him stories of the Lord and Joseph and David. All his life he had wanted a book. Now he held one in his hands, and it was only making his bruised fingers hurt more. He would carry it with him anyway.

He passed a large brick schoolhouse with big windows and children climbing on little ladders and swinging on swings. No one jeered at him or noticed him because he had crossed the street and was walking close up against the hedge on the other side. Soon the painted houses ran out, and he was walking past unpainted cabins. He always felt better on his travels when he came to the part of town where the unpainted cabins were. Sometimes people came out on the porch when he passed and talked to him. Sometimes they gave him a piece to eat on the way. Now he thought they might laugh and say "What you carryin', child? A book?" So he held it close up against him.

"That's a school too," the boy said to himself as he stood facing a small unpainted building with its door at the end instead of the side, the way cabin doors were. Besides, he could always tell a school because it had more windows than a cabin.

At the side of the building two children were sloshing water out of a tin pail near a hand pump. One threw a dipper of water on a dog that came from underneath to bark at the boy. The school was built on posts, and a stovepipe came through the wall and stuck up above the rafters. A rusty tin pipe ran from the corner of the roof down to the cistern where the children were playing.

The dog had gone back under the building, so the boy entered the yard and moved toward the children. If one of them would work the pump handle, he could wash the dried blood off his hand. Just when he reached the cistern, a wild commotion of barking burst from under the floor of the school. Half a dozen dogs, which followed children to school and waited patiently for lunch-time scraps and for school to be over, burst from under the building in pursuit of a pig that had wandered onto the lot. In the wild chase around the building the biggest dog struck the tin drain-pipe, and it clattered down the wall and bounced on the cement top of the cistern. With a pig under the building and the dogs barking and racing in and out, the school day ended.

Two dozen or more children raced out the door, few of them touching the three steps that led from the stoop to the ground. Some were calling the names of dogs and looking under the building. The boy found himself surrounded by strange inquiring eyes. Questions came too fast to answer. "You new here?" "Where you moved to?" "That your book?" "You comin' here to school?" "Kin you read that big a book?" The boy had put his bruised hand into his pocket so no one could see it. Some of the children carried books too, but none were as big as the one he held close against his side.

Just when the commotion was quieting down, a man appeared at the schoolhouse door. The children scattered across the lot in four directions. "Tell your pa that he must keep his pig in the pen," he called to one child.

Then it was quiet. The boy looked at the man in the doorway. They were alone now. The dogs had followed the children. And the pig, hearing a familiar call from the corner of the lot, had come grunting from his sanctuary and gone in the direction of the call.

In his many journeyings among strangers the boy had learned to sniff out danger and spot orneriness quickly. Now, for the first time in his life away from home, he wasn't feared. The lean elderly man with snow-white hair, wearing Sunday clothes, came down the steps. "This pipe is always falling," he said as he picked it up and put it back in place. "I need to wire it up."

"I just wanted to wash my hand. It's got dried blood on it where I hurt my fingers."

"You should have run home."

"I don't live in these parts."

"Here, I'll hold your book, and I'll pump for you." And the mellow eyes of the man began to search the boy for answers, answers that could be found without asking questions.

"We need warm soapy water," the teacher said. "I live right close. Wait 'til I get my papers and lock the door, and I'll take you home and fix it."

The boy wanted to follow the man into the schoolhouse and see what it was like inside, but by the time he got to the steps the man was back again, locking the door. "I usually put the school in order after the children leave," he said, "but I'll do it in the morning before they get here."

At the edge of the school lot the man took the road that led away from the town. They walked without much talk, and the boy began to wish the man would ask him a lot of questions. When they had passed several cabins, each farther from the other as they went, the man turned off the road and said, "We're home. I live here alone. Have lived alone for a long time." Fingering the small wire hook on the neatly whitewashed gate which led into a yard that was green, the teacher stopped talking.

A cabin with a gate and green grass in the yard is almost a big house, the boy thought as he followed the man.

Inside the gate the man went along the fence,

studying some plants tied up to stakes. He began to talk again, not to the boy, but to a plant that was smaller than the others. "You'll make it, little one, but it'll take time to get your roots set again."

The boy looked at the white-haired old man leaning over like he was listening for the plant to answer him. "He's conjured," the boy whispered to himself. "Lots of old folks is conjured or addled." He moved backward to the gate, thinking he'd better run away. "Conjured folks can conjure you," the boy's mother always said, "if you get yourself plain carried off by their soft spell-talk."

But before the boy could trouble his mind anymore, the man straightened up and began talking to him. "Some animal dug under the roots and tore them loose from the earth. It was wilted badly and might have died. But I reset it, and I water it every day. It's hard to reset a plant if it's wilted too much; the life has gone out of it. But this one will be all right. I see new leaves startin'."

"What grows on it?" the boy asked, thinking it must be something good to eat if somebody cared that much about a plant.

"It's only a flower," the man said. "I'll water it when the earth has cooled a little. If you water a plant when the earth is too warm, it shocks the roots."

Inside the cabin the man started a fire in the cookstove and heated water. As he washed the boy's hand with a soft white rag he said, "You musta slammed these fingers in a awful heavy door or gate." Before the boy could answer, the teacher began to talk about the plant he must remember to water.

He don't wanta know nothin' about me, the boy thought.

"When I saw your book, I thought you were coming to enroll for school. But you don't live in these parts, you say."

"I found the book in a trash barrel. It has words like I ain't used to readin'. I can read store-sign words and some newspaper words."

"This is a wonderful book," said the teacher. "It was written by a man named Montaigne, who was a soldier. But he grew tired of being a soldier and spent his time studying and writing. He also liked to walk on country roads."

The teacher lit two lamps. The boy had never seen two lamps burning in the same room. They made the room as bright as daylight.

"People should read his writings," the man continued. "But few do. He is all but forgotten." But the boy did not hear. He was thinking of a cabin that had two lamps, both lit at the same time, and two stoves, one to cook on and one to warm by.

The man sat in a chair between two tables that held the lamps. There were books on the tables too, and there were shelves filled not with pans and dishes, but with books. The mellow eyes of the man followed the boy's puzzled glances as they studied the strange warm world in which he had suddenly found himself.

"I will read you a little story from your book." The boy watched as the fingers of the man turned the pages one way and then the other until he found what he wanted to read.

"This is a very short story about a king named Cyrus, who wanted to buy the prize horse that belonged to one of his soldiers. Cyrus asked him how much he would sell the horse for, or whether he would exchange him for a kingdom. The soldier said he would not sell his prize horse and he would not exchange him for a kingdom, but that he would willingly give up his horse to gain a friend. . . . But now I have told you the whole story so there's no use for me to read it."

"You've been a powerful good friend to take me in like this," the boy said at last. "My fingers don't hurt no more."

"I am your friend," said the man. "So while I heat some water to soak your hand and make your cot for the night, you tell me all about yourself."

"I had a father and a dog named Sounder," the boy began. . . .

VIII

"WHO'S BEEN KINDLY to your hurts?" the boy's mother asked as she looked down at the clean white rags that bandaged the boy's fingers. Rocking on the porch, she had seen the white dot swinging back and forth in the sun when the boy wasn't much more than a moving spot far down the road. "For a while I wasn't sure it was you," she said. "Why you walkin' fast? You done found him? Is your hand hurt bad? Is that a Bible some-

99

body's done mistreated?" The woman's eyes had come to rest on the book the boy held in his good hand.

"No. It's a book. I found it in a trash can."

"Be careful what you carry off, child," his mother said. "It can cause a heap o' trouble."

"I got somethin' to tell," the boy said as he sat down on the edge of the porch and ran his bandaged fingers over the head of the great coon dog who had stopped his jumping and whining and lay at the boy's feet with his head cocked to the side, looking up with his one eye. The younger children sat in a line beside the boy, waiting to hear.

"Is he poorly?" the woman asked slowly. "Is he far?"

"It's about somethin' else," the boy said after a long spell of quiet. "I ain't found him yet."

The boy told his mother and the children about his night in the teacher's cabin. The teacher wanted him to come back and go to school. He had been asked to live in the teacher's cabin and do his chores. The children's eyes widened when they heard the cabin had two lamps, two stoves, and grass growing in a yard with a fence and a gate. He told how the teacher could read and that there were lots of books on shelves in the cabin.

100

"Maybe he will write letters to the road camps for you," the mother said, " 'cause you'll be so busy with schoolin' and cleanin' the schoolhouse for him that you can't go searchin' no more."

"Maybe I'd have time," the boy said. "But he says like you, 'Better not to go. Just be patient and time will pass.' "

"It's all powerful puzzlin' and aggravatin', but it's the Lord's will." The boy noticed that his mother had stopped rocking; the loose boards did not rattle as the chair moved on them.

"The teacher said he'd walk all the way and reason about it if you didn't want me to come to him. You don't want me to go, but I'll come home often as I can. And sometime I might bring word."

"It's a sign; I believes in signs." The rocker began to move back and forth, rattling the loose boards in the porch floor. "Go child. The Lord has come to you."

*　　　*　　　*

When he returned to the cabin with books on the shelves and the kind man with the white hair and the gentle voice, all the boy carried was his book with one cover missing—the book that he

101

couldn't understand. In the summers he came home to take his father's place in the fields, for cabin rent had to be paid with field work. In the winter he seldom came because it took "more'n a day's walkin' and sleepin' on the ground."

"Ain't worth it" his mother would say.

Each year, after he had been gone for a whole winter and returned, the faithful Sounder would come hobbling on three legs far down the road to meet him. The great dog would wag his tail and whine. He never barked. The boy sang at his work in the fields, and his mother rocked in her chair and sang on the porch of the cabin. Sometimes when Sounder scratched fleas under the porch, she would look at the hunting lantern and the empty possum sack hanging against the wall. Six crops of persimmons and wild grapes had ripened. The possums and raccoons had gathered them unmolested. The lantern and possum sack hung untouched. "No use to nobody no more," the woman said.

The boy read to his brother and sisters when he had finished his day in the fields. He read the story of Joseph over and over and never wearied of it. "In all the books in the teacher's cabin, there's no story as good as Joseph's story" he would say to them.

The woman, listening and rocking, would say "The Lord has come to you, child. The Lord has certainly come to you."

Late one August afternoon the boy and his mother sat on the shaded corner of the porch. The heat and drought of dog days had parched the earth, and the crops had been laid by. The boy had come home early because there was nothing to do in the fields.

"Dog days is a terrible time," the woman said. "It's when the heat is so bad the dogs go mad." The boy would not tell her that the teacher had told him that dog days got their name from the Dog Star because it rose and set with the sun during that period. She had her own feeling for the earth, he thought, and he would not confuse it.

"It sure is hot," he said instead. "Lucky to come from the fields early." He watched the heat waves as they made the earth look like it was moving in little ripples.

Sounder came around the corner of the cabin from somewhere, hobbled back and forth as far as the road several times, and then went to his cool spot under the porch. "That's what I say about dog days," the woman said. "Poor creature's been addled with the heat for three days. Can't find no place to quiet down. Been down the road

103

nearly out o' sight a second time today, and now he musta come from the fencerows. Whines all the time. A mad dog is a fearful sight. Slobberin' at the mouth and runnin' every which way 'cause they're blind. Have to shoot 'em 'fore they bite some child. It's awful hard."

"Sounder won't go mad," the boy said. "He's lookin' for a cooler spot, I reckon."

A lone figure came on the landscape as a speck and slowly grew into a ripply form through the heat waves. "Scorchin' to be walkin' and totin' far today," she said as she pointed to the figure on the road.

A catbird fussed in the wilted lilac at the corner of the cabin. "Why's that bird fussin' when no cat's prowlin? Old folks has a sayin' that if a catbird fusses 'bout nothin', somethin' bad is comin'. It's a bad sign."

"Sounder, I reckon," the boy said. "He just passed her bush when he came around the cabin."

In the tall locust at the edge of the fence, its top leaves yellowed from lack of water, a mockingbird mimicked the catbird with half a dozen notes, decided it was too hot to sing, and disappeared. The great coon dog, whose rhythmic panting came through the porch floor, came from under the house and began to whine.

As the figure on the road drew near, it took shape and grew indistinct again in the wavering heat. Sometimes it seemed to be a person dragging something, for little puffs of red dust rose in sulfurous clouds at every other step. Once or twice they thought it might be a brown cow or mule, dragging its hooves in the sand and raising and lowering its weary head.

Sounder panted faster, wagged his tail, whined, moved from the dooryard to the porch and back to the dooryard.

The figure came closer. Now it appeared to be a child carrying something on its back and limping.

"The children still at the creek?" she asked.

"Yes, but it's about dry."

Suddenly the voice of the great coon hound broke the sultry August deadness. The dog dashed along the road, leaving three-pointed clouds of red dust to settle back to earth behind him. The mighty voice rolled out upon the valley, each flutelike bark echoing from slope to slope.

"Lord's mercy! Dog days done made him mad." And the rocker was still.

Sounder was a young dog again. His voice was the same mellow sound that had ridden the November breeze from the lowlands to the hills. The boy and his mother looked at each other. The catbird stopped her fussing in the wilted lilac bush. On three legs, the dog moved with the same lightning speed that had carried him to the throat of a grounded raccoon.

Sounder's master had come home. Taking what might have been measured as a halting half step and then pulling a stiff, dead leg forward, dragging a foot turned sideways in the dust, the man limped into the yard. Sounder seemed to understand that to jump up and put his paw against his master's breast would topple him into the dust, so the great dog smelled and whined and wagged his tail and licked the limp hand dangling at his master's side. He hopped wildly around his master in a circle that almost brought head and tail together.

The head of the man was pulled to the side where a limp arm dangled and where the foot pointed outward as it was dragged through the dust. What had been a shoulder was now pushed up and back to make a one-sided hump so high that the leaning head seemed to rest upon it. The mouth was askew too, and the voice came out of the part farthest away from the withered, wrinkled, lifeless side.

The woman in the still rocker said, "Lord, Lord," and sat suffocated in shock.

"Sounder knew it was you just like you was comin' home from work," the boy said in a clear voice.

Half the voice of the man was gone too, so in slow, measured, stuttering he told how he had been caught in a dynamite blast in the prison quarry, how the dead side had been crushed under an avalanche of limestone, and how he had been missed for a whole night in the search for dead and wounded. He told how the pain of the crushing stone had stopped in the night, how doctors had pushed and pulled and encased the numb side of his body in a cast, how they had spoken kindly to him and told him he would die. But he resolved he would not die, even with a half-dead body, because he wanted to come home again.

"For being hurt, they let me have time off my sentence," the man said, "and since I couldn't work, I guess they was glad to."

"The Lord has brought you home," the woman said.

The boy heard faint laughter somewhere behind the cabin. The children were coming home from the creek. He went around the cabin slowly, then hurried to meet them.

"Pa's home," he said and grabbed his sister,

108

who had started to run toward the cabin. "Wait. He's mighty crippled up, so behave like nothin' has happened."

"Can he walk?" the youngest child asked.

"Yes! And don't you ask no questions."

"You been mighty natural and considerate," the mother said to the younger children later when she went to the woodpile and called them to pick dry kindling for a quick fire. When she came back to the porch she said, "We was gonna just have a cold piece 'cause it's so sultry, but now I think I'll cook."

Everything don't change much, the boy thought. There's eatin' and sleepin' and talkin' and settin' that goes on. One day might be different from another, but there ain't much difference when they're put together.

Sometimes there were long quiet spells. Once or twice the boy's mother said to the boy, "He's powerful proud of your learnin'. Read somethin' from the Scriptures." But mostly they just talked about heat and cold, and wind and clouds, and what's gonna be done, and time passing.

As the days of August passed and September brought signs of autumn, the crippled man sat on the porch step and leaned the paralyzed, deformed side of his body against a porch post. This was the only comfortable sitting position he could find. The old coon dog would lie facing his master, with his one eye fixed and his one ear raised. Sometimes he would tap his tail against the earth. Sometimes the ear would droop and the eye would close. Then the great muscles would flex in dreams of the hunt, and the mighty chest would give off the muffled whisper of a bark. Sometimes the two limped together to the edge of the fields, or wandered off into the pine woods. They never went along the road. Perhaps they knew how strange a picture they made when they walked together.

About the middle of September the boy left to go back to his teacher. "It's the most important thing," his mother said.

And the crippled man said, "We're fine. We won't need nothin'."

"I'll come for a few days before it's cold to help gather wood and walnuts."

The broken body of the old man withered more and more, but when the smell of harvest and the hunt came with October, his spirit seemed to quicken his dragging step. One day he cleaned the dusty lantern globe, and the old dog, remembering, bounced on his three legs and wagged his tail as if to say "I'm ready."

The boy had come home. To gather the felled trees and chop the standing dead ones was part of

110

the field pay too. He had been cutting and dragging timber all day.

Sometimes he had looked longingly at the lantern and possum sack, but something inside him had said "Wait. Wait and go together." But the boy did not want to go hunting anymore. And without his saying anything, his father had said, "You're too tired, child. We ain't goin' far, no way."

In the early darkness the halting, hesitant swing of the lantern marked the slow path from fields to pine woods toward the lowlands. The boy stood on the porch, watching until the light was lost behind pine branches. Then he went and sat by the stove. His mother rocked as the mound of kernels grew in the fold of her apron. "He been mighty peart," she said. "I hope he don't fall in the dark. Maybe he'll be happy now he can go hunting again." And she took up her singing where she had left off.

> *Ain't nobody else gonna walk it for you,*
> *You gotta walk it by yourself.*

* * *

Sounder's scratching at the door awakened the boy. It was still night, but the first red glow of

111

dawn was rising in a faint crescent over the pine woods.

"Sounder just couldn't poke slow enough for your father," the mother said to the boy as they stood in the doorway, straining and sifting the dark for some movement.

"Lantern wouldn't burn out in this time," the boy said. "No sign of light. He must have fallen or got tired. Sounder will show me."

Sounder was already across the road into the stalk land, whining, moving his head from one side to the other, looking back to be sure that the boy was following.

Across the stalk land, into the pine woods, into the climbing, brightening glow of the dawn, the boy followed the dog, whose anxious pace slowed from age as they went. "By a dog's age, Sounder is past dying time," the boy said half aloud. Fear had always prompted him to talk to himself.

Deep in the pine woods, along a deserted logging road, the boy and dog came to a small open space where there had once been a log ramp. The sun was just beginning to drive its first splinters of light through the pines, bouncing against tree trunks and earth. At the foot of one of the trees the boy's father sat, the lantern still burning by his side.

"So tuckered out he fell asleep," the boy said to himself.

But the figure did not move when Sounder licked his hand. The boy put his hand on his father's good shoulder and shook ever so gently. The chin did not lift itself; no eyes turned up to meet the boy. "Tired, so tired."

When the boy returned to the cabin and told his mother, her lips grew long and thin and pale. But when she finally spoke, they were warm and soft as when she sang. "When life is so tiresome, there ain't no peace like the greatest peace—the peace of the Lord's hand holding you. And he'll have a store-bought box for burial 'cause all these years I paid close attention to his burial insurance."

They buried the boy's father in the unfenced lot behind the meetin' house. The preacher stood amid the sumac and running briars before the mound of fresh red earth and read:

> The Lord is my shepherd; I shall not want,
> He maketh me to lie down in green pastures.

*   *   *

"There's plenty of wood, and I must go back to school," the boy told his mother several days after

113

they had buried his father. "Sounder ain't got no spirit left for living. He hasn't gone with me to the woods to chop since Pa died. He doesn't even whine anymore. He just lies on his coffee sacks under the cabin steps. I've dug a grave for him under the big jack oak tree in the stalk land by the fencerow. It'll be ready if the ground freezes. You can carry him on his coffee sacks and bury him. He'll be gone before I come home again."

And the boy was right. Two weeks before he came home for Christmas, Sounder crawled under the cabin and died. The boy's mother told him all there was to tell.

"He just crawled up under the house and died," she said.

The boy was glad. He had learned to read his book with the torn cover better now. He had read in it: "Only the unwise think that what has changed is dead." He had asked the teacher what it meant, and the teacher had said that if a flower blooms once, it goes on blooming somewhere forever. It blooms on for whoever has seen it blooming. It was not quite clear to the boy then, but it was now.

Years later, walking the earth as a man, it would all sweep back over him, again and again, like an echo on the wind.

The pine trees would look down forever on a lantern burning out of oil but not going out. A harvest moon would cast shadows forever of a man walking upright, his dog bouncing after him. And the quiet of the night would fill and echo again with the deep voice of Sounder, the great coon dog.

CONNECTIONS

The father in Sounder *claims that he never found, or "got,"* Sounder, *but that* Sounder *came to him. This story describes another dog who chooses his own family. Are Lob and Sounder treated differently by their human families?*

Lob's Girl
Joan Aiken

Some people choose their dogs, and some dogs choose their people. The Pengelly family had no say in the choosing of Lob; he came to them in the second way, and very decisively.

It began on the beach, the summer when Sandy was five, Don, her older brother, twelve, and the twins were three. Sandy was really Alexandra, because her grandmother had a beautiful picture of a queen in a diamond tiara and high collar of pearls. It hung by Granny Pearce's kitchen sink and was as familiar as the doormat. When Sandy was born everyone agreed that she was the living spit of the picture, and so she was called Alexandra and Sandy for short.

On this summer day she was lying peacefully reading a comic and not keeping an eye on the twins, who didn't need it because they were occupied in seeing which of them could wrap the most seaweed around the other one's legs. Father— Bert Pengelly—and Don were up on the Hard painting the bottom boards of the boat in which Father went fishing for pilchards. And Mother—Jean Pengelly—was getting ahead with making the Christmas puddings because she never felt easy in her mind if they weren't made and safely put away by the end of August. As usual, each member of the family was happily getting on with his or her own affairs. Little did they guess how soon this state of things would be changed by the large new member who was going to erupt into their midst.

Sandy rolled onto her back to make sure that the twins were not climbing on slippery rocks or getting cut off by the tide. At the same moment a large body struck her forcibly in the midriff and she was covered by flying sand. Instinctively she shut her eyes and felt the sand being wiped off her face by something that seemed like a warm, rough, damp flannel. She opened her eyes and looked. It was a tongue. Its owner was a large and bouncy young Alsatian, or German shepherd, with topaz eyes, black-tipped prick ears, a thick, soft coat, and a bushy black-tipped tail. *"Lob!"* shouted a man farther up the beach. "Lob, come here!"

But Lob, as if trying to atone for the surprise he had given her, went on licking the sand off Sandy's face, wagging his tail so hard while he kept on knocking up more clouds of sand. His owner, a gray-haired man with a limp, walked over as quickly as he could and seized him by the collar.

"I hope he didn't give you a fright?" the man said to Sandy. "He meant it in play—he's only young."

"Oh, no, I think he's *beautiful*," said Sandy truly. She picked up a bit of driftwood and threw it. Lob, whisking easily out of his master's grip, was after it like a sand-colored bullet. He came back with the stick, beaming, and gave it to Sandy. At the same time he gave himself, though no one else was aware of this at the time. But with Sandy, too, it was love at first sight, and when, after a lot more stick-throwing, she and the twins joined Father and Don to go home for tea, they cast many a backward glance at Lob being led firmly away by his master.

"I wish we could play with him every day." Tess sighed.

"Why can't we?" said Tim.

Sandy explained. "Because Mr. Dodsworth, who owns him, is from Liverpool, and he is only staying at the Fisherman's Arms till Saturday."

"Is Liverpool a long way off?"

"Right at the other end of England from Cornwall, I'm afraid."

It was a Cornish fishing village where the Pengelly family lived, with rocks and cliffs and a strip of beach and a little round harbor, and palm trees growing in the gardens of the little whitewashed stone houses. The village was approached by a narrow, steep, twisting hill-road, and guarded by a notice that said LOW GEAR FOR 1½ MILES, DANGEROUS TO CYCLISTS.

The Pengelly children went home to scones with Cornish cream and jam, thinking they had seen the last of Lob. But they were much mistaken. The whole family was playing cards by the fire in the front room after supper when there was a loud thump and a crash of china in the kitchen.

"My Christmas puddings!" exclaimed Jean, and ran out.

"Did you put TNT in them, then?" her husband said.

But it was Lob, who, finding the front door shut, had gone around to the back and bounced in through the open kitchen window, where the puddings were cooling on the sill. Luckily only the smallest was knocked down and broken.

Lob stood on his hind legs and plastered Sandy's face with licks. Then he did the same for the twins, who shrieked with joy.

"Where does this friend of yours come from?" inquired Mr. Pengelly.

"He's staying at the Fisherman's Arms—I mean his owner is."

"Then he must go back there. Find a bit of string, Sandy, to tie to his collar."

"I wonder how he found his way here," Mrs. Pengelly said, when the reluctant Lob had been led whining away and Sandy had explained about their afternoon's game on the beach. "Fisherman's Arms is right round the other side of the harbor."

Lob's owner scolded him and thanked Mr. Pengelly for bringing him back. Jean Pengelly warned the children that they had better not encourage Lob any more if they met him on the beach, or it would only lead to more trouble. So they dutifully took no notice of him the next day until he spoiled their good resolutions by dashing up to them with joyful barks, wagging his tail so hard that he winded Tess and knocked Tim's legs from under him.

They had a happy day, playing on the sand.

The next day was Saturday. Sandy had found out that Mr. Dodsworth was to catch the half-past-nine train. She went out secretly, down to the station, nodded to Mr. Hoskins, the stationmaster, who wouldn't dream of charging any local for a platform ticket, and climbed up on the footbridge that led over the tracks. She didn't want to be seen, but she did want to see. She saw Mr. Dodsworth get on the train, accompanied by an unhappy-looking Lob with drooping ears and tail. Then she saw the train slide away out of sight around the next headland, with a melancholy wail that sounded like Lob's last good-bye.

Sandy wished she hadn't had the idea of coming to the station. She walked home miserably, with her shoulders hunched and her hands in her pockets. For the rest of the day she was so cross and unlike herself that Tess and Tim were quite surprised, and her mother gave her a dose of senna.

A week passed. Then, one evening, Mrs. Pengelly and the younger children were in the front room playing snakes and ladders. Mr. Pengelly and Don had gone fishing on the evening tide. If your father is a fisherman, he will never be home at the same time from one week to the next.

Suddenly, history repeating itself, there was a crash from the kitchen. Jean Pengelly leaped up, crying, "My blackberry jelly!" She and the children had spent the morning picking and the afternoon boiling fruit.

But Sandy was ahead of her mother. With flushed cheeks and eyes like stars she had darted into the kitchen, where she and Lob were hugging one another in a frenzy of joy. About a yard of his tongue was out, and he was licking every part of her that he could reach.

"Good heavens!" exclaimed Jean. "How in the world did *he* get here?"

"He must have walked," said Sandy. "Look at his feet."

They were worn, dusty, and tarry. One had a cut on the pad.

"They ought to be bathed," said Jean Pengelly. "Sandy, run a bowl of warm water while I get the disinfectant."

"What'll we do about him, Mother?" said Sandy anxiously.

Mrs. Pengelly looked at her daughter's pleading eyes and sighed.

"He must go back to his owner, of course," she said, making her voice firm. "Your dad can get the address from the Fisherman's tomorrow, and phone him or send a telegram. In the meantime he'd better have a long drink and a good meal."

Lob was very grateful for the drink and the meal, and made no objection to having his feet washed. Then he flopped down on the hearthrug and slept in front of the fire they had lit because it was a cold, wet evening, with his head on Sandy's feet. He was a very tired dog. He had walked all the way from Liverpool to Cornwall, which is more than four hundred miles.

The next day Mr. Pengelly phoned Lob's owner, and the following morning Mr. Dodsworth arrived off the night train, decidedly put out, to take his pet home. That parting was worse than the first. Lob whined, Don walked out of the house, the twins burst out crying, and Sandy crept up to her bedroom afterward and lay with her face pressed into the quilt, feeling as if she were bruised all over.

Jean Pengelly took them all into Plymouth to see the circus on the next day and the twins cheered up a little, but even the hour's ride in the train each way and the Liberty horses and performing seals could not cure Sandy's sore heart.

She need not have bothered, though. In ten days' time Lob was back—limping this time, with a torn ear and a patch missing out of his furry coat, as if he had met and tangled with an enemy or two in the course of his four-hundred-mile walk.

Bert Pengelly rang up Liverpool again. Mr. Dodsworth, when he answered, sounded weary. He said, "That dog has already cost me two days that I can't spare away from my work—plus endless time in police stations and drafting newspaper advertisements. I'm too old for these ups and downs. I think we'd better face the fact, Mr. Pengelly, that it's your family he wants to stay with—that is, if you want to have him."

Bert Pengelly gulped. He was not a rich man; and Lob was a pedigreed dog. He said cautiously, "How much would you be asking for him?"

"Good heavens, man, I'm not suggesting I'd *sell* him to you. You must have him as a gift. Think of the train fares I'll be saving. You'll be doing me a good turn."

"Is he a big eater?" Bert asked doubtfully.

By this time the children, breathless in the background listening to one side of this conversation, had realized what was in the wind and were dancing up and down with their hands clasped beseechingly.

"Oh, not for his size," Lob's owner assured Bert. "Two or three pounds of meat a day and some vegetables and gravy and biscuits—he does very well on that."

Alexandra's father looked over the telephone at his daughter's swimming eyes and trembling lips. He reached a decision. "Well, then, Mr. Dodsworth," he said briskly, "we'll accept your offer and thank you very much. The children will be overjoyed and you can be sure Lob has come to a good home. They'll look after him and see he gets enough exercise. But I can tell you," he ended firmly, "if he wants to settle in with us he'll have to learn to eat a lot of fish."

So that was how Lob came to live with the Pengelly family. Everybody loved him and he loved them all. But there was never any question who came first with him. He was Sandy's dog. He slept by her bed and followed her everywhere he was allowed.

Nine years went by, and each summer Mr. Dodsworth came back to stay at the Fisherman's Arms and call on his erstwhile dog. Lob always met him with recognition and dignified pleasure, accompanied him for a walk or two—but showed no signs of wishing to return to Liverpool. His place, he intimated, was definitely with the Pengellys.

In the course of nine years Lob changed less than Sandy. As she went into her teens he became a little slower, a little stiffer, there was a touch of gray on his nose, but he was still a handsome dog. He and Sandy still loved one another devotedly.

One evening in October all the summer visitors had left, and the little fishing town looked empty and secretive. It was a wet, windy dusk. When the children came home from school— even the twins were at high school now, and Don was a full-fledged fisherman—Jean Pengelly said, "Sandy, your Aunt Rebecca says she's lonesome because Uncle Will Hoskins has gone out trawling, and she wants one of you to go and spend the evening with her. You go, dear; you can take your homework with you."

Sandy looked far from enthusiastic.

"Can I take Lob with me?"

"You know Aunt Becky doesn't really like dogs—Oh, very well." Mrs. Pengelly sighed. "I suppose she'll have to put up with him as well as you."

Reluctantly Sandy tidied herself, took her schoolbag, put on the damp raincoat she had just taken off, fastened Lob's lead to his collar, and set off to walk through the dusk to Aunt Becky's cottage, which was five minutes' climb up the steep hill.

The wind was howling through the shrouds of boats drawn up on the Hard.

"Put some cheerful music on, do," said Jean Pengelly to the nearest twin. "Anything to drown that wretched sound while I make your dad's supper." So Don, who had just come in, put on some rock music, loud. Which was why the Pengellys did not hear the truck hurtle down the hill and crash against the post office wall a few minutes later.

Dr. Travers was driving through Cornwall with his wife, taking a late holiday before patients began coming down with winter colds and flu. He saw the sign that said STEEP HILL. LOW GEAR FOR 1½ MILES. Dutifully he changed into second gear.

"We must be nearly there," said his wife, looking out of her window. "I noticed a sign on the coast road that said the Fisherman's Arms was two miles. What a narrow, dangerous hill! But the cottages are very pretty—Oh, Frank, stop, *stop!* There's a child, I'm sure it's a child—by the wall over there!"

Dr. Travers jammed on his brakes and brought the car to a stop. A little stream ran down by the road in a shallow stone culvert, and half in the water lay something that looked, in the dusk, like a pile of clothes—or was it the body of a child? Mrs. Travers was out of the car in a flash, but her husband was quicker.

"Don't touch her, Emily!" he said sharply. "She's been hit. Can't be more than a few minutes. Remember that truck that overtook us half a mile back, speeding like the devil? Here, quick, go into that cottage and phone for an ambulance. The girl's in a bad way. I'll stay here and do what I can to stop the bleeding. Don't waste a minute."

Doctors are expert at stopping dangerous bleeding, for they know the right places to press. This Dr. Travers was able to do, but he didn't dare do more; the girl was lying in a queerly crumpled heap, and he guessed she had a number of bones

126

broken and that it would be highly dangerous to move her. He watched her with great concentration, wondering where the truck had got to and what other damage it had done.

Mrs. Travers was very quick. She had seen plenty of accident cases and knew the importance of speed. The first cottage she tried had a phone; in four minutes she was back, and in six an ambulance was wailing down the hill.

Its attendants lifted the child onto a stretcher as carefully as if she were made of fine thistledown. The ambulance sped off to Plymouth—for the local cottage hospital did not take serious accident cases—and Dr. Travers went down to the police station to report what he had done.

He found that the police already knew about the speeding truck—which had suffered from loss of brakes and ended up with its radiator halfway through the post office wall. The driver was concussed and shocked, but the police thought he was the only person injured—until Dr. Travers told his tale.

At half-past nine that night Aunt Rebecca Hoskins was sitting by her fire thinking aggrieved thoughts about the inconsiderateness of nieces who were asked to supper and never turned up, when she was startled by a neighbor, who burst in, exclaiming, "Have you heard about Sandy Pengelly, then, Mrs. Hoskins? Terrible thing, poor little soul, and they don't know if she's likely to live. Police have got the truck driver that hit her—ah, it didn't ought to be allowed, speeding through the place like that at umpty miles an hour, they ought to jail him for life—not that that'd be any comfort to poor Bert and Jean."

Horrified, Aunt Rebecca put on a coat and went down to her brother's house. She found the family with white shocked faces; Bert and Jean were about to drive off to the hospital where Sandy had been taken, and the twins were crying bitterly. Lob was nowhere to be seen. But Aunt Rebecca was not interested in dogs; she did not inquire about him.

"Thank the lord you've come, Beck," said her brother. "Will you stay the night with Don and the twins? Don's out looking for Lob and heaven knows when we'll be back; we may get a bed with Jean's mother in Plymouth."

"Oh, if only I'd never invited the poor child," wailed Mrs. Hoskins. But Bert and Jean hardly heard her.

That night seemed to last forever. The twins cried themselves to sleep. Don came home very late and grim-faced. Bert and Jean sat in a waiting room of the Western Counties Hospital, but Sandy was unconscious, they were told, and she remained so. All that could be done for her was done. She was given transfusions to replace all the blood she had lost. The broken bones were set and put in slings and cradles.

"Is she a healthy girl? Has she a good constitution?" the emergency doctor asked.

"Aye, doctor, she is that," Bert said hoarsely. The lump in Jean's throat prevented her from answering; she merely nodded.

"Then she ought to have a chance. But I won't conceal from you that her condition is very serious, unless she shows signs of coming out from this coma."

But as hour succeeded hour, Sandy showed no signs of recovering consciousness. Her parents sat in the waiting room with haggard faces; sometimes one of them would go to telephone the family at home, or to try to get a little sleep at the home of Granny Pearce, not far away.

At noon next day Dr. and Mrs. Travers went to the Pengelly cottage to inquire how Sandy was doing, but the report was gloomy: "Still in a very serious condition." The twins were miserably unhappy. They forgot that they had sometimes called their elder sister bossy and only remembered how often she had shared her pocket money with them, how she read to them and took them for picnics and helped with their homework. Now there was no Sandy, no Mother and Dad, Don went around with a gray, shuttered face, and worse still, there was no Lob.

The Western Counties Hospital is a large one, with dozens of different departments and five or six connected buildings, each with three or four entrances. By that afternoon it became noticeable that a dog seemed to have taken up position outside the hospital, with the fixed intention of getting in. Patiently he would try first one entrance and then another, all the way around, and then begin again. Sometimes he would get a little way inside, following a visitor, but animals were, of course, forbidden, and he was always kindly but firmly turned out again. Sometimes the guard at the main entrance gave him a pat or offered him a bit of sandwich—he looked so wet and beseeching and desperate. But he never ate the sandwich. No one seemed to own him or to know where he came from; Plymouth is a large city and he might have belonged to anybody.

At tea time Granny Pearce came through the pouring rain to bring a flask of hot tea with brandy in it to her daughter and son-in-law. Just as she reached the main entrance the guard was gently but forcibly shoving out a large, agitated, soaking-wet Alsatian dog.

"No, old fellow, you can *not* come in. Hospitals are for people, not for dogs."

"Why, bless me," exclaimed old Mrs. Pearce. "That's Lob! Here, Lob, Lobby boy!"

Lob ran to her, whining. Mrs. Pearce walked up to the desk.

"I'm sorry, madam, you can't bring that dog in here," the guard said.

Mrs. Pearce was a very determined old lady. She looked the porter in the eye.

"Now, see here, young man. That dog has walked twenty miles from St. Killan to get to my granddaughter. Heaven

knows how he knew she was here, but it's plain he knows. And
he ought to have his rights! He ought to get to see her! Do you
know," she went on, bristling, "that dog has walked the length
of England—*twice*—to be with that girl? And you think you can
keep him out with your fiddling rules and regulations?"

"I'll have to ask the medical officer," the guard said weakly.

"You do that, young man." Granny Pearce sat down in
a determined manner, shutting her umbrella, and Lob sat
patiently dripping at her feet. Every now and then he shook
his head, as if to dislodge something heavy that was tied
around his neck.

Presently a tired, thin, intelligent-looking man in a white
coat came downstairs, with an impressive, silver-haired man in a
dark suit, and there was a low-voiced discussion. Granny Pearce
eyed them, biding her time.

"Frankly . . . not much to lose," said the older man. The
man in the white coat approached Granny Pearce.

"It's strictly against every rule, but as it's such a serious case
we are making an exception," he said to her quietly. "But only
outside her bedroom door—and only for a moment or two."

Without a word, Granny Pearce rose and stumped upstairs.
Lob followed close to her skirts, as if he knew his hope lay
with her.

They waited in the green-floored corridor outside Sandy's
room. The door was half shut. Bert and Jean were inside.
Everything was terribly quiet. A nurse came out. The white-
coated man asked her something and she shook her head. She
had left the door ajar and through it could now be seen a high,
narrow bed with a lot of gadgets around it. Sandy lay there,
very flat under the covers, very still. Her head was turned away.
All Lob's attention was riveted on the bed. He strained toward
it, but Granny Pearce clasped his collar firmly.

"I've done a lot for you, my boy, now you behave yourself,"

she whispered grimly. Lob let out a faint whine, anxious and pleading.

At the sound of that whine Sandy stirred just a little. She sighed and moved her head the least fraction. Lob whined again. And then Sandy turned her head right over. Her eyes opened, looking at the door.

"Lob?" she murmured—no more than a breath of sound. "Lobby, boy?"

The doctor by Granny Pearce drew a quick, sharp breath. Sandy moved her left arm—the one that was not broken— from below the covers and let her hand dangle down, feeling, as she always did in the mornings, for Lob's furry head. The doctor nodded slowly.

"All right," he whispered. "Let him go to the bedside. But keep a hold of him."

Granny Pearce and Lob moved to the bedside. Now she could see Bert and Jean, white-faced and shocked, on the far side of the bed. But she didn't look at them. She looked at the smile on her granddaughter's face as the groping fingers found Lob's wet ears and gently pulled them. "Good boy," whispered Sandy, and fell asleep again.

Granny Pearce led Lob out into the passage again. There she let go of him and he ran off swiftly down the stairs. She would have followed him, but Bert and Jean had come out into the passage, and she spoke to Bert fiercely.

"*I* don't know why you were so foolish as not to bring the dog before! Leaving him to find the way here himself—"

"But, Mother!" said Jean Pengelly. "That can't have been Lob. What a chance to take! Suppose Sandy hadn't—" She stopped, with her handkerchief pressed to her mouth.

"Not Lob? I've known that dog nine years! I suppose I ought to know my own granddaughter's dog?"

"Listen, Mother," said Bert. "Lob was killed by the same

131

truck that hit Sandy. Don found him—when he went to look for Sandy's schoolbag. He was—he was dead. Ribs all smashed. No question of that. Don told me on the phone—he and Will Hoskins rowed a half mile out to sea and sank the dog with a lump of concrete tied to his collar. Poor old boy. Still—he was getting on. Couldn't have lasted forever."

"*Sank him at sea?* Then what—?"

Slowly old Mrs. Pearce, and then the other two, turned to look at the trail of dripping-wet footprints that led down the hospital stairs.

In the Pengellys' garden they have a stone, under the palm tree. It says: "Lob. Sandy's dog. Buried at sea."

■ ■ ■

*The bond between Sounder and his human family is very
strong, but also very mysterious—we never know exactly what
gives him the strength to return to the family home. What do
you think could create bonds between dogs and humans that
are as strong as the ones described in these selections?*

The Smartest Human I Ever Met: My Brother's Dog Shep
Victor Villaseñor

I was eight years old the night my brother's dog went crazy-
loco and started racing around the house, howling to the
heavens. It was late at night, I was sound asleep, and my
parents were down in San Diego at Scripps Hospital seeing
my brother, who'd been sick for nearly a year. Joseph was
sixteen years old, and he'd been hit in a football game and
just bruised a little bit internally, but our local doctor—a
drunk—hadn't attended to him correctly, and his liver was
ruined and he developed leukemia.

I could hear his dog Shep racing around the house, howling like crazy. Quickly, I got up to go see what was the matter.
Shep was a very smart dog and didn't bark for just any reason.
I pulled on my boots and got my BB gun and went out the
front door. There was a half-moon and the stars were out by
the thousands. We lived on a ranch in north San Diego County
not far from the sea, and often animals came down the canyon
behind our home on their way to the ocean. I looked around
but saw nothing. As far as I could see, the dog was just chasing around after himself, acting crazy. I called him.

"Shep!" I shouted to him. "It's all right. Just come in.
Nothing's the matter."

I wanted him to come to me so I could pet him and calm

him down, but he wouldn't come near me. No, he just kept racing around and howling like he was *loco*. And Shep was a smart, level-headed dog, too. He was half coyote and half Shepherd and I'd been hunting and going horseback riding with him for as long as I could remember. He'd always listened to me before, so I couldn't figure out what was going on. He was acting really strange. He just kept racing around and around the house, howling something fierce.

My little sister Linda woke up and came outside to see what was the matter, too. Then, the Mexican-Indian woman, Rosa, who was taking care of us while my parents were gone, came outside to check on us.

"Is everything all right?" asked Rosa in Spanish. We all spoke Spanish on the ranch. English wasn't a language any of us spoke unless we went out the gates of the property.

"Yes," I said in Spanish, "It's just that our dog has gone crazy. He's barking at nothing and won't come to me."

"He's not barking at nothing," Rosa said to me. "He's barking because your brother is dying."

I was stunned. I didn't know what to think. "But my brother isn't dying," I said. "He's getting well. That's why my parents have him in the hospital."

Rosa's husband, Emilio, suddenly came out of the dark, and I now saw that several other of the farmhands were all sitting quietly under the huge pepper tree.

"Rosa is right," he said gently. "Your brother is dying. That's why his dog is going crazy; he loves your brother very much."

"Yes, he loves my brother, but, well," I stopped. I didn't know what to say. My parents had told my sister and me that they had the best doctors money could buy attending to my brother, and that he was getting well. I glanced from Emilio to Rosa and then back again. "But how can this dog know that my brother is dying? My brother is more than thirty miles away! You're wrong! You're wrong! You just don't know what you're talking about!"

"All right," said Emilio, putting his arm about his wife's shoulders, "have it your way. But understand, the soul knows no distance, and love speaks through the heart. And that dog is telling us of his heart breaking for your brother."

"No!" I yelled. "My brother isn't dying! Shep has got to stop howling!"

But no matter how much I yelled at him, Shep wouldn't stop. I began to cry, too. I was scared now, and my heart was breaking, just like Shep's.

The workmen never said a thing. They just sat there under the huge pepper tree, poking at the ground with sticks and being very quiet. Rosa finally took my sister and me back inside.

All that night, my brother's dog kept howling, and then, in the early morning, he suddenly stopped, just like that. When I went outside to see what had happened, I was told that he'd taken off for the hills.

My parents came home later that day and informed my sister and me that our brother Joseph had died. They said that the doctors had done all they could with their modern medicine, but still he was gone.

I could see that mother's whole face was swollen from crying when she went into the house. My father stayed out-side with my sister and me. I wanted to tell my father that we'd found out about my brother's death the night before because of his dog, but I just didn't know how to say this without sounding stupid.

Later that day, I went to tell Emilio and Rosa that they were right, that my brother had died, but they said they already knew.

"We saw his dog take off this morning for the hills to intercept his soul," said Rosa.

I'll never forget the chills that went up and down my spine on hearing those words "to intercept his soul," and I got this powerful image of my brother's dog running up to the highest hilltop he could find and leaping into the sky to join with my brother's soul as it made its way to heaven.

We never saw my brother's dog after that. And when I asked Rosa and her husband what had happened to Shep, they explained to me that he'd left his body up in the hills somewhere so he could travel to the other side of life with my brother, whom he'd loved very much. Animals, she'd explained to me, could do that at will, much easier than humans, because they hadn't learned how to talk and question yet, and love was still their basis for living life.

Shortly after that, Rosa and Emilio returned to Mexico. They left a couple of days after I told my father of the things that they'd told me about Shep and my brother. My dad got real angry and said, "Your mother and I got the finest doctor we could find for your brother, and no stupid old Indian beliefs are going to create doubt of my word!"

But, no matter how much my father raged and shouted, I still knew that I'd seen my brother's dog go crazy-*loco* with his love for my brother and then disappear the next day to never be seen again.

Moco Limping
David Nava Monreal

My dog hobbles
with a stick
of a leg that
he drags behind
him as he moves.
And I was a man
that wanted a
beautiful, noble
animal as a pet.
I wanted him
to be strong and
capture all the
attention by
the savage grace
of his gait.
I wanted him to
be the first
dog howling in
the pack.
The leader,
the brutal hunter
that broke through
the woods with
thunder.
But, instead
he's this rickety

little canine
that leaves trails
in the dirt
with his club foot.
He's the stumbler
that trips while
chasing lethargic
bees and butterflies.
It hurts me to
see him so
abnormal,
so clumsy and
stupid.
My vain heart weeps
knowing he
is mine.
But then he turns
my way and
looks at me with
eyes that cry out
with life.
He jumps at me with
his feeble paws.
I feel his warm fur
and his imperfection is forgotten.

■ ■ ■

An absent father, a son on a journey to find him—it sounds like
Sounder, doesn't it? This story takes place far from the world of
Sounder's sharecropping family, but there are still some surprising
similarities. What are the different burdens that the sons in these
two stories have to bear?

Spirits of the Railway
Paul Yee

One summer many, many years ago, heavy floodwaters suddenly swept through south China again. Farmer Chu and his
family fled to high ground and wept as the rising river drowned
their rice crops, their chickens and their water buffalo.

With their food and farm gone, Farmer Chu went to town
to look for work. But a thousand other starving peasants were
already there. So when he heard there was work across the
ocean in the New World, he borrowed some money, bought a
ticket, and off he sailed.

Long months passed as his family waited to hear from him.
Farmer Chu's wife fell ill from worry and weariness. From her
hard board bed she called out her husband's name over and
over, until at last her eldest son borrowed money to cross the
Pacific in search of his father.

For two months, young Chu listened to waves batter the
groaning planks of the ship as it crossed the ocean. For two
months he dreaded that he might drown at any minute. For
two months he thought of nothing but his father and his family.

Finally he arrived in a busy port city. He asked everywhere
for his father, but no one in Chinatown had heard the name.
There were thousands of Chinese flung throughout the New
World, he was told. Gold miners scrabbled along icy rivers,

farmers ploughed the long low valleys, and laborers traveled through towns and forests, from job to job. Who could find one single man in this enormous wilderness?

Young Chu was soon penniless. But he was young and strong, and he feared neither danger nor hard labor. He joined a work gang of thirty Chinese, and a steamer ferried them up a river canyon to build the railway.

When the morning mist lifted, Chu's mouth fell open. On both sides of the rushing river, gray mountains rose like walls to block the sky. The rock face dropped into ragged cliffs that only eagles could ascend and jutted out from cracks where scrawny trees clung. Never before had he seen such towering ranges of dark raw rock.

The crew pitched their tents and began to work. They hacked at hills with hand-scoops and shovels to level a pathway for the train. Their hammers and chisels chipped boulders into gravel and fill. Their dynamite and drills thrust tunnels deep into the mountain. At night, the crew would sit around the campfire chewing tobacco, playing cards and talking.

From one camp to another, the men trekked up the rail line, their food and tools dangling from sturdy shoulder poles. When they met other workers, Chu would run ahead and shout his father's name and ask for news. But the workers just shook their heads grimly.

"Search no more, young man!" one grizzled old worker said. "Don't you know that too many have died here? My own brother was buried alive in a mudslide."

"My uncle was killed in a dynamite blast," muttered another. "No one warned him about the fuse."

The angry memories rose and swirled like smoke among the workers.

"The white boss treats us like mules and dogs!"

"They need a railway to tie this nation together, but they

can't afford to pay decent wages."

"What kind of country is this?"

Chu listened, but still he felt certain that his father was alive.

Then winter came and halted all work. Snows buried everything under a heavy blanket of white. The white boss went to town to live in a warm hotel, but Chu and the workers stayed in camp. The men tied potato sacks around their feet and huddled by the fire, while ice storms howled like wolves through the mountains. Chu thought the winter would never end.

When spring finally arrived, the survivors struggled outside and shook the chill from their bones. They dug graves for two workers who had succumbed to sickness. They watched the river surge alive from the melting snow. Work resumed, and Chu began to search again for his father.

Late one afternoon, the gang reached a mountain with a half-finished tunnel. As usual, Chu ran up to shout his father's name, but before he could say a word, other workers came running out of the tunnel.

"It's haunted!" they cried. "Watch out! There are ghosts inside!"

"Dark figures slide soundlessly through the rocks!" one man whispered. "We hear heavy footsteps approaching but never arriving. We hear sighs and groans coming from corners where no man stands."

Chu's friends dropped their packs and refused to set up camp. But the white boss rode up on his horse and shook his fist at the men. "No work, no pay!" he shouted. "Now get to work!"

Then he galloped off. The workers squatted on the rocks and looked helplessly at one another. They needed the money badly for food and supplies.

Chu stood up. "What is there to fear?" he cried. "The ghosts have no reason to harm us. There is no reason to be afraid. We have hurt no one."

"Do you want to die?" a man called out.

"I will spend the night inside the tunnel," Chu declared as the men muttered unbelievingly. "Tomorrow we can work."

Chu took his bedroll, a lamp, and food and marched into the mountain. He heard the crunch of his boots and water dripping. He knelt to light his lamp. Rocks lay in loose piles everywhere, and the shadowy walls closed in on him.

At the end of the tunnel he sat down and ate his food. He closed his eyes and wondered where his father was. He pictured his mother weeping in her bed and heard her voice calling his father's name. He lay down, pulled his blankets close, and eventually he fell asleep.

Chu awoke gasping for breath. Something heavy was pressing down on his chest. He tried to raise his arms but could not. He clenched his fists and summoned all his strength, but still he was paralyzed. His eyes strained into the darkness, but saw nothing.

Suddenly the pressure eased and Chu groped for the lamp. As the chamber sprang into light, he cried, "What do you want? Who are you?"

Silence greeted him, and then a murmur sounded from behind. Chu spun around and saw a figure in the shadows. He slowly raised the lamp. The flickering light traveled up blood-stained trousers and a mud-encrusted jacket. Then Chu saw his father's face.

"Papa!" he whispered, lunging forward.

"No! Do not come closer!" The figure stopped him. "I am not of your world. Do not embrace me."

Tears rose in Chu's eyes. "So, it's true," he choked. "You . . . you have left us . . ."

His father's voice quivered with rage. "I am gone, but I am not done yet. My son, an accident here killed many men.

A fuse exploded before the workers could run. A ton of rock dropped on us and crushed us flat. They buried the whites in a churchyard, but our bodies were thrown into the river, where the current swept us away. We have no final resting place."

Chu fell upon his knees. "What shall I do?"

His father's words filled the tunnel. "Take chopsticks; they shall be our bones. Take straw matting; that can be our flesh. Wrap them together and tie them tightly. Take the bundles to the mountain top high above the nests of eagles, and cover us with soil. Pour tea over our beds. Then we shall sleep in peace."

When Chu looked up, his father had vanished. He stumbled out of the tunnel and blurted the story to his friends. Immediately they prepared the bundles and sent him off with ropes and a shovel to the foot of the cliff, and Chu began to climb.

When he swung himself over the top of the cliff, he was so high up that he thought he could see the distant ocean. He dug the graves deeper than any wild animal could dig, and laid the bundles gently in the earth.

Then Chu brought his fists together above his head and bowed three times. He knelt and touched his forehead to the soil three times. In a loud clear voice he declared, "Three times I bow, three things I vow. Your pain shall stop now, your sleep shall soothe you now, and I will never forget you. Farewell."

Then, hanging onto the rope looped around a tree, Chu slid slowly back down the cliff. When he reached the bottom, he looked back and saw that the rope had turned into a giant snake that was sliding smoothly up the rock face.

"Good," he smiled to himself. "It will guard the graves well." Then he returned to the camp, where he and his fellow workers lit their lamps and headed into the tunnel. And spirits never again disturbed them, nor the long trains that came later.

■ ■ ■

The boy in Sounder *finally learns to read, but just a few decades earlier, in the years of slavery, he might never have had the chance. Think about that fact as you read this section of the autobiography of Frederick Douglass, who escaped from slavery when he was a young man. Would you have taken the risks that Douglass did?*

Learning to Read and Write
from The Narrative of the
Life of Frederick Douglass

I lived in Master Hugh's family about seven years. During this time, I succeeded in learning to read and write. In accomplishing this, I was compelled to resort to various stratagems. I had no regular teacher. My mistress, who had kindly commenced to instruct me, had, in compliance with the advice and direction of her husband, not only ceased to instruct, but had set her face against my being instructed by any one else. It is due, however, to my mistress to say of her, that she did not adopt this course of treatment immediately. She at first lacked the depravity indispensable to shutting me up in mental darkness. It was at least necessary for her to have some training in the exercise of irresponsible power, to make her equal to the task of treating me as though I were a brute.

My mistress was, as I have said, a kind and tender-hearted woman; and in the simplicity of her soul she commenced, when I first went to live with her, to treat me as she supposed one human being ought to treat another. In entering upon the duties of a slaveholder, she did not seem to perceive that I sustained to her the relation of a mere chattel, and that for her to treat me as a human being was not only wrong, but dangerously so. Slavery proved as injurious to her as it did to me. When I went there, she was a pious, warm, and tender-hearted woman. There was no sorrow or suffering for which she had not a tear. She had bread for the hungry, clothes for the naked, and comfort for every mourner that came within her reach. Slavery soon proved its ability to divest her of these heavenly qualities. Under its influence, the tender heart became stone, and the lamblike disposition gave way to one of tiger-like fierceness. The first step in her downward course was in her ceasing to instruct me. She now commenced to practise her husband's precepts. She finally became even more violent in her opposition than her husband himself. She was not satisfied with simply doing as well as he had commanded; she seemed anxious to do better. Nothing seemed to make her more angry than to see me with a newspaper. She seemed to think that here lay the danger. I have had her rush at me with a face made all up of fury, and snatch from me a newspaper, in a manner that fully revealed her apprehension. She was an apt woman; and a little experience soon demonstrated, to her satisfaction, that education and slavery were incompatible with each other.

From this time I was most narrowly watched. If I was in a separate room any considerable length of time, I was sure to be suspected of having a book, and was at once called to give an account of myself. All this, however, was too late. The first step had been taken. Mistress, in teaching me the alphabet, had given me the *inch,* and no precaution could prevent me from taking the *ell.*

The plan which I adopted, and the one by which I was most successful, was that of making friends of all the little white boys whom I met in the street. As many of these as I could, I converted into teachers. With their kindly aid, obtained at different times and in different places, I finally suc-

ceeded in learning to read. When I was sent of errands,
I always took my book with me, and by going one part of
my errand quickly, I found time to get a lesson before my
return. I used also to carry bread with me, enough of which
was always in the house and to which I was always welcome;
for I was much better off in this regard than many of the poor
white children in our neighborhood. This bread I used to
bestow upon the hungry little urchins, who, in return, would
give me that more valuable bread of knowledge. I am strongly
tempted to give the names of two or three of those little boys,
as a testimonial of the gratitude and affection I bear them; but
prudence forbids;—not that it would injure me, but it might
embarrass them; for it is almost an unpardonable offence to
teach slaves to read in this Christian country. It is enough to
say of the dear little fellows, that they lived on Philpot Street,
very near Durgin and Bailey's ship-yard. I used to talk this
matter of slavery over with them. I would sometimes say to
them, I wished I could be as free as they would be when
they got to be men. "You will be free as soon as you are
twenty-one, *but I am a slave for life!* Have not I as good a right
to be free as you have?" These words used to trouble them;
they would express for me the liveliest sympathy, and console
me with the hope that something would occur by which I
might be free.

I was now about twelve years old, and the thought of
being a *slave* for *life* began to bear heavily upon my heart.
Just about this time, I got hold of a book entitled "The
Columbian Orator." Every opportunity I got, I used to read
this book. Among much of other interesting matter, I found
in it a dialogue between a master and his slave. The slave
was represented as having run away from his master three
times. The dialogue represented the conversation which took
place between them, when the slave was retaken the third

time. In this dialogue, the whole argument in behalf of slavery was brought forward by the master, all of which was disposed of by the slave. The slave was made to say some very smart as well as impressive things in reply to his master—things which had the desired though unexpected effect; for the conversation resulted in the voluntary emancipation of the slave on the part of the master.

In the same book, I met with one of Sheridan's mighty speeches on and in behalf of Catholic emancipation. These were choice documents to me. I read them over and over again with unabated interest. They gave tongue to interesting thoughts of my own soul, which had frequently flashed through my mind, and died away for want of utterance. The moral which I gained from the dialogue was the power of truth over the conscience of even a slaveholder. What I got from Sheridan was a bold denunciation of slavery, and a powerful vindication of human rights. The reading of these documents enabled me to utter my thoughts, and to meet the arguments brought forward to sustain slavery; but while they relieved me of one difficulty, they brought on another even more painful than the one of which I was relieved. The more I read, the more I was led to abhor and detest my enslavers. I could regard them in no other light than a band of successful robbers, who had left their homes, and gone to Africa, and stolen us from our homes, and in a strange land reduced us to slavery. I loathed them as being the meanest as well as the most wicked of men. As I read and contemplated the subject, behold! that very discontentment which Master Hugh had predicted would follow my learning to read had already come, to torment and sting my soul to unutterable anguish. As I writhed under it, I would at times feel that learning to read had been a curse rather than a blessing. It had given me a view of my wretched condition, without the remedy. It opened my eyes to the horrible pit, but to no ladder upon which to get out. In moments of agony, I envied my fellow-slaves for their stupidity. I have often wished myself a beast. I preferred the condition of the meanest reptile to my own. Any thing, no matter what, to get rid of thinking! It was this everlasting thinking of my condition that tormented me. There was no getting rid of it. It was pressed upon me by every object within sight or hearing, animate or inanimate. The silver trump of freedom had roused my soul to eternal wakefulness. Freedom now appeared, to disappear no more forever. It was heard in every sound, and seen in every thing. It was ever present to torment me with a sense of my wretched condition. I saw nothing without seeing it, I heard nothing without hearing it, and felt nothing without feeling it. It looked from every star, it smiled in every calm, breathed in every wind, and moved in every storm.

I often found myself regretting my own existence, and wishing myself dead; and but for the hope of being free, I have no doubt but that I should have killed myself, or done something for which I should have been killed. While in this state of mind, I was eager to hear any one speak of slavery. I was a ready listener. Every little while, I could hear something about the abolitionists. It was some time before I found what the word meant. It was always used in such connections as to make it an interesting word to me. If a slave ran away and succeeded in getting clear, or if a slave killed his master, set fire to a barn, or did anything very wrong in the mind of a slaveholder, it was spoken of as the fruit of *abolition*. Hearing the word in this connection very often, I set about learning what it meant. The dictionary afforded me little or no help. I found it was "the act of abolishing"; but then I did not know what was to be abolished. Here I was perplexed. I did not dare to ask any one about its meaning, for I was satisfied that it was something they wanted me to know very little about. After a patient waiting, I got one of our city papers, containing an account of the number of petitions from the north, praying for the abolition of slavery in the District of Columbia, and of the slave trade between the States. From this time I understood the words *abolition* and *abolitionist*, and always drew near when that word was spoken, expecting to hear something of importance to myself and fellow-slaves. The light broke in upon me by degrees. I went one day down on the wharf of Mr. Waters; and seeing two Irishmen unloading a scow of stone, I went, unasked, and helped them. When we had finished, one of them came to me and asked me if I were a slave. I told him I was. He asked, "Are ye a slave for life?" I told him that I was. The good Irishman seemed to be deeply affected by the statement. He said to the other that it was a pity so fine a little fellow as myself should be a slave for life. He said it was a shame to hold me. They both advised me to run away to the north; that I should find friends there, and that I should be free. I pretended not to be interested in what they said, and treated them as if I did not understand them; for I feared they might be treacherous. White men have been known to encourage slaves to escape, and then, to get the reward, catch them and return them to their masters. I was afraid that these seemingly good men might use me so; but I nevertheless remembered their advice, and from that time I resolved to run away. I looked forward to a time at which it would be safe for me to escape. I was too young to think of doing so immediately; besides, I wished to learn how to write, as I might have occasion to write my own pass. I consoled myself with the hope that I should one day find a good chance. Meanwhile, I would learn to write.

The idea as to how I might learn to write was suggested to me by being in Durgin and Bailey's ship-yard, and frequently seeing the ship carpenters, after hewing, and getting a piece of timber ready for use, write on the timber the name of that part of the ship for which it was intended. When a piece of timber was intended for the larboard side, it would be marked thus— "L." When a piece was for the starboard side, it would be marked thus—"S." A piece for the larboard side forward, would be marked thus—"L.F." When a piece was for starboard side forward, it would be marked thus—"S.F." For larboard aft, it would be marked thus—"L.A." For starboard aft, it would be marked thus—"S.A." I soon learned the names of these letters, and for what they were intended when placed upon a piece of timber in the ship-yard. I immediately commenced copying them, and in a short time was able to make the four letters named. After that, when I met with any boy who I knew could write, I would tell him I could write as well as he. The next word would be, "I don't believe you. Let me see you try it." I would then make the letters which I had been so fortunate as to learn, and ask him to beat that. In this way I got a good many lessons in writing, which it is quite possible I should never have gotten in any other way. During this time, my copy-book was the board fence, brick wall, and pavement; my pen and ink was a lump of chalk. With these, I learned mainly how to write. I then commenced and continued copying the Italics in Webster's Spelling Book, until I could make them all without looking on the book. By this time, my little Master Thomas had gone to school, and learned how to write, and had written over a number of copy-books. These had been brought home, and shown to some of our near neighbors, and then laid aside. My mistress used to go to class meeting at the Wilk Street meeting-house every Monday afternoon, and leave me to take care of the house. When left thus, I used to spend the time in writing in the spaces left in Master Thomas's copy-book, copying what he had written. I continued to do this until I could write a hand very similar to that of Master Thomas. Thus, after a long, tedious effort for years, I finally succeeded in learning how to write.

■ ■ ■

In Sounder, *the boy's mother often sings an old spritual called "Lonesome Valley" while she works. Here are the words to "Lonesome Valley" and to a more recent song. In what ways are these two songs alike?*

Lonesome Valley

You got to walk that lonesome valley,
You got to walk it by yourself,
Ain't nobody here can walk it for you,
You got to walk that lonesome valley by yourself.

Your mother's got to walk that lonesome valley,
She got to walk it by herself,
Ain't nobody here can walk it for her,
She got to walk that lonesome valley by herself.

Your father's got to walk that lonesome valley,
He got to walk it by himself,
Ain't nobody here can walk it for him,
He got to walk that lonesome valley by himself.

Your brother's got to walk that lonesome valley,
He got to walk it by himself,
Ain't nobody here can walk it for him,
He got to walk that lonesome valley by himself.

If you cannot preach like Peter,
If you cannot pray like Paul,
You can tell the love of Jesus,
You can say He died for all.

I Believe I Can Fly
R. Kelly

I used to think that I could not go on,
and life was nothing but an awful song.
But now I know the meaning of true love.
I'm leaning on the everlasting arm.

If I can see it, then I can do it,
if I just believe it, there's nothing to it.
I believe I can fly, I believe I can touch the sky.
I think about it every night and day,
spread my wings and fly away.
I believe I can soar,
I see me running through that open door.
I believe I can fly,
I believe I can fly,
I believe I can fly.

See, I was on the verge of breaking down.
Sometimes silence can seem so loud.
There are miracles in life I must achieve,
but first I know it starts inside of me.

If I can see it, then I can be it,
if I just believe it, there's nothing to it.
I believe I can fly, I believe I can touch the sky.
I think about it every night and day,
spread my wings and fly away.

I believe I can soar,
I see me running through that open door.
I believe I can fly,
I believe I can fly,
I believe I can fly,
oh, I believe I can fly.

Hey, 'cause I believe in me, oh.
If I can see it, then I can do it,
if I just believe it, there's nothing to it.
I believe I can fly, I believe I can touch the sky.
I think about it every night and day,
spread my wings and fly away.
I believe I can soar,
I see me running through that open door.
I believe I can fly,
I believe I can fly,
I believe I can fly,
hey, if I just spread my wings.
I can fly, I can fly, I can fly,
hey, if I just spread my wings.
I can fly.

■ ■ ■

As he searches the prisons and work gangs for his father, the boy in
Sounder *thinks about the story of David and Goliath from the Bible.
This version of the story is written as a play, so you can read it aloud
with some classmates. Think about why the boy in* Sounder *might
identify with a character from this story.*

David and Goliath
from I Samuel 17
adapted by Diane B. Engel

READER 1:   Now the Philistines gathered their armies to
            battle . . .

READER 2:   . . . and Saul and the men of Israel gathered
            together, and prepared to battle the Philistines.

READER 1:   The Philistines stood on a mountain on one side,

READER 2:   and Israel stood on a mountain on the other side,
            with a valley between them.

READER 1:   And out of the camp of the Philistines there came a
            champion, named—

ALL: Goliath of Gath—

READER 1:   —whose height was six cubits and a span.

READER 3:   He had a helmet of brass on his head, and he was
            armed with a coat of mail that weighed five thousand
            shekels of brass.

READER 4:   And he had plates of brass upon his legs and
            between his shoulders.

READER 3:   The staff of his spear was like a weaver's beam; and the head of his spear weighed six hundred shekels of iron; and one went before him, carrying his shield.

READER 4:   And the champion of the Philistines stood and cried unto the armies of Israel, and said unto them:

TRIO: "Why have you come out to do battle? Am I not a Philistine, and you are servants of Saul? Choose someone to represent you, and let him come to me.

"If he can fight with me, and kill me, then we will be your servants; but if I prevail against him, then you will be our servants, and serve us.

"I defy the armies of Israel this day: Give me a man, that we may fight together!"

READER 2:   When Saul and all Israel heard those words of the Philistine, they were dismayed, and greatly afraid.

READER 5:   Now David was the son of Jesse of Bethlehem, who had eight sons. His three eldest sons went and followed Saul into battle. David was the youngest, and he stayed in Bethlehem to take care of his father's sheep.

ALL: And the Philistine drew near, morning and evening, for forty days.

READER 1:   One day Jesse sent David to visit his brothers in the camp. And as he talked with them—behold, the champion came—

ALL: —the Philistine of Gath, Goliath by name—

READER 1:   —and he spoke his challenge, and David heard it. And all the men of Israel, when they saw the man, fled from him, and were deeply afraid.

READER 5: David spoke to the men around him, "Who is this unbelieving Philistine, that he should defy the armies of the living God?"

READER 2: When word of this came to Saul, he sent for David. And David said to Saul, "Let no one be afraid. I, your servant, will go and fight this Philistine."

READER 3: Saul said to David, "You cannot go against this Philistine, to fight with him! You are only a youth— and he has been a man of war from his youth."

READER 5: And David replied, "I used to take care of my father's sheep. Whenever a lion or a bear came and took a lamb out of the flock, I went out after him, and struck him, and saved the lamb. If he attacked me, I caught him by his fur and killed him.

"I have killed both lions and bears. This un-believing Philistine will be like them, for he has defied the armies of the living God. The Lord, who delivered me from the paw of the lion and the paw of the bear, will deliver me from the hand of this Philistine."

READER 3: Saul said to David, "Go, and may the Lord be with you." And Saul dressed David in his own armor, and put a brass helmet on his head, and armed him with his coat of mail.

READER 5: But David said to Saul, "I cannot go with these, for I have not proved myself worthy to wear them." So David removed the armor.

READER 2: Instead, David took own his staff, and he chose five smooth stones out of the brook, and put them in his shepherd's bag. With his sling in his hand, he drew near to the Philistine.

READER 4: And the Philistine came on and drew near to David; and the man who carried his shield went before him. And when the Philistine looked about and saw David, he disdained him, for David was but a youth. And the Philistine said to David,

TRIO: "Am I a dog, that you come to me with sticks?"

READER 4: And the Philistine cursed David to his gods. Then he said to David,

TRIO: "Come to me! I will give your flesh to the fowls of the air and to the beasts of the field!"

READER 5: Then David said to the Philistine, "You come to me with a sword, and a spear, and a shield; but I come to you in the name of the Lord of Hosts, the God of the armies of Israel, whom you have defied.

"This day the Lord will deliver you into my hand. I will strike you and take your head from you; and I will give the carcasses of the host of the Philistines today to the fowls of the air, and to the wild beasts of the earth; that all the earth may know that there is a God in Israel. And all who are assembled here will know that the Lord does not save with sword or spear; this battle is the Lord's, and He will give you into our hands."

READER 1: And it came to pass, when the Philistine arose, and drew near to meet David,

READER 2: that David ran toward the army to meet the Philistine. And David put his hand into his bag, and took a stone, and fired it from his sling—

TRIO: —and struck the Philistine in the forehead, that the stone sank into his forehead; and he fell upon his face to the earth.

READER 2: So David prevailed over the Philistine with a sling and a stone! He struck the Philistine and killed him; but there was no sword in the hand of David.

READER 5: So David ran and stood upon the Philistine. He took the sword, and drew it out of its sheath, and killed the Philistine, and cut off his head.

READER 1: When the Philistines saw that their champion was dead, they fled.

READER 3: And the men of Israel and Judah arose and shouted; and they pursued the Philistines.

ALL: And David took the head of the Philistine and brought it to Jerusalem.

■ ■ ■

William H. Armstrong

■ (Born 1914) ■

A writer, teacher, and farmer, William H. Armstrong grew up on a farm in the Shenandoah Valley of Virginia. His childhood there was steeped in a profound awareness of the history of his home region. More than one Sunday school teacher reminded him that he sat in a church where Stonewall Jackson, the Confederate general, had taught Sunday school. (The Shenandoah Valley was also the stage for several battles of the Civil War, and the Confederate general Robert E. Lee spent the last years of his life near Armstrong's hometown.)

None of this history was lost on Armstrong. After three years at a military academy, he studied history at Hampden-Sydney College and in graduate school at the University of Virginia. He then took a job teaching history at the Kent School in Kent, Connecticut, where he lived for more than forty years.

Armstrong began writing history books and study guides in the 1950s. Then, one evening as he walked beside the Housatonic River near Kent, the idea for *Sounder* came to him. As he told it later, the quiet of the night made him wonder about a legendary hunting dog he had been told about years before.

> Was the October night's song lasting enough to let a lone walker's ears pick up the faint, distant voice of Sounder, the great coon dog, a voice the stroller in the night had never heard, but had only heard about, so many years ago . . . ?

Armstrong had been told the story of Sounder by a family friend, an African American man who had taught him to read. The early life of this quiet, eloquent man was a fascinating mystery to Armstrong, and he used the story of Sounder as a way to explore one possible version of his friend's childhood.

The idea lay dormant for a long while. "[M]ost of my books," Armstrong explains, "begin with an idea that I take inside and keep there for a long time before I write a single word. It gets into my blood and is filtered through my heart until it is a part of me. *Sounder* . . . was filtered through my heart about four years before any writing except a few notes on three-by-five cards."

Armstrong finished *Sounder* in the winter of 1969, writing mostly in the mornings before sunrise. He wrote quickly—the novel was finished before winter ended—but he let it sit on a shelf for a while. Finally, one day in March, he finally decided to release his story into the world. "I saw my neighbor sawing wood across the fence. I climbed the fence, crossed his brook, and asked him to read my story."